STONE MEN

A CHARLES BLOOM MURDER MYSTERY

MARK SUBLETTE

Mark Sublette

 JUST ME PUBLISHING

Copyright © 2014 by Mark Sublette
Author's Note by Mark Sublette Copyright © 2014

All Rights Reserved. This book may not be reproduced, in whole or in part, in any form, without written permission. For inquiries, contact: Just Me Publishing, LLC., Tucson, AZ, 1-800-422-9382

Published by Just Me Publishing, LLC.

Library of Congress Control Number: 2014942222
Stone Men / Mark Sublette
ISBN 978-0-9855448-7-4
1. Fiction I. Title

Quantity Purchases
Companies, professional groups, clubs, and other organizations may qualify for special terms when ordering quantities of this title. For more information, contact us through www.marksublette.com.

Cover painting: Josh Elliott, *Sunset Moonrise*
Jacket and book design: Jaime Gould
Author photo: Dan Budnik

Printed in the USA by Bookmasters
Ashland, OH · www.bookmasters.com

AUTHOR'S NOTE

The books in the Bloom murder mystery series are all works of fiction. The CXI Corporation and its mine are fictional, however the turquoise grades mentioned other than #35 are all real. This book is dedicated to those individuals who have spent their lives in search of the next great stone.

All the characters are fictional as are all the police officers, FBI agents, art galleries, artists and art dealers. The Native American characters in my book are fictional and any resemblance by name, clan, or description to real life is pure coincidence.

The Toadlena Trading Post, a central component of all the Bloom books, is a real-life working trading post that exists as described on Navajoland. This historic post specializes in Toadlena/Two Grey Hills weavings and is well worth the effort to visit. I would like to thank its proprietor, author Mark Winter, and his wife Linda, for their invaluable insight and Mark's careful editing prowess.

No book is complete with out a great cover and I'm most appreciative to Josh Elliott for so graciously allowing me to use SUNSET MOONRISE to capture the essence of the Navajo Reservation and to Jaime Gould for her graphic design skills.

I must thank two stone men: John Miller, who lives for the find and took time to share his knowledge, and Doug Magnus, whose guided tour through his beloved Cerrillos Mine outside of Santa Fe and studio provided invaluable reference.

All the photographs of Santa Fe, Tucson, and Navajoland are taken by me and serve as points of reference that correlate to each chapter. Hopefully they help to give the reader the sense of place and moment in time that I experienced when I took them.

CHAPTER 1

#35

The stone man's hand trembled slightly as he inspected his precious find. Endorphins pulsed through his body, a rare occurrence for an ex-Marine who understood true danger. The catalyst of his excitement wasn't a bullet, but a colorful rock shaped like an oversized deer pellet. It was the moment he lived for, the thrill of finding a new turquoise deposit. It had been two years since his last adrenaline surge. Now it was 2014 and he had found the mother lode. His tremulous hand told the whole story.

The President, as he was known in the world of rock hounds, had made a monumental discovery. It was the finest raw turquoise nugget he had ever seen, and a surface find at that. The probability was that there were plenty more precious veins of turquoise just underneath the bare Navajo sandstone. It had taken good detective work, years of experience in the field, but now it was going to pay off big-time. Most stone men, even good ones, would have breezed past, never giving the nondescript pebble a second glance.

Not the President. His well-trained eye discerned the glint of importance nestled in a tan sandstone trough, one of thousands of ravines that made up this portion of the Navajo Nation. Here it was in his hand. A magic pill, the panacea for all that ails a hard-lived life. A rough turquoise stone that would transform his remaining time and solidify his standing as the best in the field. And not a moment too soon. Still vital and standing six-foot-two, the President was nonetheless in his mid-sixties and knew his tough days trudging through sandy terrain under a searing sun seeking a miracle find would soon give way to mortality's mandates.

The stone was on Navajo property but private land was less than a quarter-mile away. He would just stretch the truth a bit on its location, a specialty of the trade.

The President managed to muster a little saliva, which he applied to the nugget. Its true beauty came shining through. Gingerly he rolled the precious stone between his thumb and index finger, instinctively gauging its value. Reticulated silver encapsulations appeared on the rough stone, the same glint that initially caught his attention. To the trained eye, its structure was visible even without magnification. It was a flawless gem. The rock's complex metallic matrix deposited in a sea of aquamarine color was an exceptional mix of silver and blue. The stone was no larger than a marble, but after cutting and polishing it would result in two small five-carat cabochons. He would realize an astronomical premium, the most any turquoise had ever demanded. He figured out loud, "$500 a carat has a nice ring to it," computing what his eyes confirmed. He already had a name picked out, one he been saving for the ultimate turquoise find. A moniker worthy of his own initials, JFK, also the initials of the 35th president of the US.

"#35, my search is over. You will make #8 look like a second-grade gem stone," he told his new stone, laughing at the thought of his new discovery outclassing #8, which up until this point was considered probably the premium-grade turquoise. "I'm going to always price you at almost double the spot value of #8," he planned, his booming voice echoing off the steep white walls of the canyon.

As the last of his voice trailed off into distant Navajoland, the President heard a new sound reverberate through the high desert air. It was the crack of a high-power rifle, a noise he knew. The President ducked his head and turned instinctively. A second later he felt an excruciating pain burn through his right triceps, his precious

#35 escaping his grip, bouncing one time before plummeting down a bottomless crevice, lost forever to mankind. The only colored stone now was the crimson sandstone slab he was laying on, blood oozing over the rocks he loved so much.

The President had hit the ground with an audible thud, like a kill shot to a deer. His left thigh was bruised and swelling, but his quick action had saved his life. A second shot whizzed 10 inches over his head, ricocheting off a boulder and almost hitting him in the back. He began gasping rapidly. It was hard to focus, but if he wanted to live he knew exactly what he had to do. Two years in 'Nam had taught him how to survive. This wasn't his first go-round at being shot. It appeared his arm had only suffered a flesh wound. His truck was hidden a quarter-mile away and dusk was in a half-hour. He could tell by the sound of the shots and the time they took to hit his arm and sweep over his head that the shooter must be fairly distant, a good marksman no doubt. It was open range and the assassin couldn't know he was unarmed, so they would be cautious, especially if they knew his history.

If the President played his cards right, he could escape. His bruised leg was usable. His arm hurt like shit but the bleeding was already slowing and he had full movement. Still a lucky day.

He managed to tuck himself behind two dinosaur-egg shaped boulders. There would be no way the shooter could hit him if he didn't panic. Keeping as low as possible, he flattened his body like a lizard in the cold. A third shot rang out, its distance as far away as the other two, bouncing around, but he was safe.

Then his unrelenting trained eye caught the reflection of something...*silver*. The low sun's rays grazed the surface of an unusual rock. His prone position gave him the optimal angle for discovery. If he were the type of man to contemplate his situation, he would stay perfectly still, but he wasn't that man. Instead, he eased his left hand out past the protective boulders, expecting to be shot, waiting for a new searing pain. Neither occurred. With slabs for fingers he trapped a golf-ball size stone that was wedged underneath two large sandstone rock formations, quickly retrieving it. Another #35!

He couldn't help but smile, admiring the gem's encryptions laced with silver. He rubbed it with his blood-soaked shirtsleeve, the deep blue color indisputable even through his own red filter. It would be worth a fortune.

There was a reason he was top of the heap, dealing in the big stones and bigger clients. But finding an entire new mine would elevate him into a different league, one where his vision and perseverance were recognized by all and financial pressures evaporated. Now if he could only figure out a way to survive so he could realize his payday. He tucked the stone safely in his shirt pocket, covered his wound, and waited for dark. No one was stealing his claim. No one.

CHAPTER 2

FEBRUARY 7-8, CUT AND POLISH

The President waited. Apparently, whoever had shot him had enough respect not to try and approach closer after winging him. The evening turned into night, the air silent except for the sound of a distant coyote pack celebrating a kill. The irony was not lost on the man stuck under his dinosaur-egg hideout.

Slowly, the President retreated out of the canyon, inching toward his truck. He knew from his time in 'Nam to go slow even if his instinct was to run. He accessed the highest point that he could in order to survey the general area of his truck. Three hours had passed. Whoever had ambushed him must have gone back the same way they came in, on foot.

Once he decided that he was in the clear, he hurried to his vehicle at a fast clip, February's cold-cutting air mitigating the prospects of any unwelcome rattlesnakes in the dark night.

Safely inside the cab of his truck, the President slumped in the driver's seat, locked the door, and pulled away his shirt for a look. The exposed meaty wound looked semi-serious but not life threatening, a nasty scar, nothing more. A quick sling and light tourniquet from an old sweat-stained shirt eased the throbbing pain and he felt a wave of relief. He had an intense urge to pull out and examine the #35 stone, but a pat of his front pocket was all the reassurance he needed. It was all his.

Driving without light made the backcountry escape more dangerous then he liked, but it was a necessary risk. Some 35 minutes later, he finally found the hardtop. Once his headlights were on, the President floored it, all the while scanning his rearview mirror and taking a circuitous route home just in case. No one followed.

Pulling up to his Gallup homestead, he observed the surrounding environment. It appeared unoccupied. He parked his truck down an adjacent street, then hurried back and slipped in the back door.

A quick survey found nothing out of place. He laid down on his bed to rest and immediately passed out on top of the blankets, not getting up until the morning light raked through the window, bringing him back to the present.

Blood had soaked through his homemade bandage and left a pink stain on the bedspread. The stain irritated the President as he should have changed his bandage first but exhaustion had gotten the better of him. He wasn't 40 anymore. Or even 50. An extra-strong cup of coffee was required.

He drank it straight and refilled his cup, then headed directly to his favorite thinking spot, a concrete bench with an old orange-red 1920s Ganado rug next to a lava fireplace hearth. For the first time since putting his arm into a sling, he took another look. The old paisley shirt from the bed of his pickup truck had made a nice sling and bandage. There was no fresh blood. All in all, it looked pretty good for being shot, better than it had last night. Sure, he had lost some blood and had a headache to go along with his aching arm, but it was a clean wound for the most part. The bleeding must have stopped shortly after he fell asleep. The wound was limited to the middle head of his right triceps muscle. Still, his arm was weak and it hurt like hell. Making a fist or straightening his arm all the way was difficult, but otherwise it seemed OK. The 10-inch scar which he estimated he would eventually have, would make a great story in the annals of stone men, assuming whoever was looking for him didn't find him first.

Without getting up, he reached out his left arm and dragged the old honey-colored Mexican pine table towards him, its legs screeching on the Saltillo tile floor, leaving marks. He placed his favorite blue coffee mug down. The words emblazoned on its side—*Bad Ass Motherfucker*—fit him well. He smiled, knowing they were still true.

After warming his left hand on the cup, he finally pulled out the large turquoise rock, which was still in his front shirt pocket. The nugget made an audible clunk on the ancient pine tabletop as it came to rest. The stone was beautiful, even in its raw state, more silver than blue. It was what his dreams were about, finding a mother lode of gem-grade turquoise. It was his future.

It was also the cause of his current predicament. He rocked the stone between his thick, callused left hand and the table, and pondered his next move. Each time he rolled the hard, uneven surface of the stone, it left a small indentation on the soft wood. It was a very dense stone. He replayed the last three months in his mind for a clue as to who had tried to kill him.

OK, stone men, we're tough, put the hurt on someone, sure, but not the murdering type, doesn't add up.

Who knew my whereabouts, two people, maybe?

Weeks of searching… plenty of time to be spotted. Could it have been that Navajo I met, Begay, who said he owned the land? Maybe wanting one less white man trespassing and stealing his family's wealth? He has a motive.

The President considered the chances of the Navajo landowner being the culprit. It didn't add up. There had been plenty of time and better places to dispose of him during the recent weeks. Yesterday's fading light was not optimal and a man who had grown up on the land would have intimate knowledge of the perfect place to kill him, probably not using a gun, preferring a boulder or dynamite.

The first shot occurred directly after I opened my mouth. It was the yell! I was being followed. Shit, I can't believe I did that.

He realized it was his own fault for shouting. He knew it was a foolish act, a slip-up for a man with a strong sense of self-preservation who liked to stay under the radar, but it had been an emotional release. He couldn't help himself. The find of a lifetime, pure joy, at a time when his body was past its prime. For someone to have been following him with his not knowing it also meant that the assassin had a unique skill set, one that had allowed him to follow a dangerous prey and not be observed: a hunter of men, probably ex-military like the President.

The throbbing in his arm returned, reminding him there was still the task of cleaning the wound—not something he was looking forward to. He didn't have any pain pills but did possess a bottle of Jack. The President was not a heavy drinker, unlike most stone men, and knew it would be a mistake to get drunk. He had made enough mistakes in the last 24 hours. He needed to focus and prioritize his next move. Gulping down a burning shot of Jack, he replayed the possibilities once more before undertaking the unpleasant task of scrubbing the wound. The booze mixed with the caffeine hit the mark.

Whoever shot me was a good enough detective to find me in Navajoland. Shit, it won't take long to track me down in Gallup either.

The sudden realization that someone was probably on his trail at this very moment sent a shiver down his spine. He slammed another shot of Jack, enough to take the edge off the wound and the situation.

Looking down at the bloody makeshift sling, the President realized there were some pressing problems. He needed to treat his arm wound. No doctors. Any medical visit would generate an automatic investigation. Wound cleaning had to be fast, and the next immediate stop should be Leroy's Lancaster's Lapidary Shop to cut and polish the raw nugget, which would allow him to raise some significant money and be able to lay low until he figured out a game plan for survival. He had $7,500 in cash but that might not be enough. He needed to pad his bank account if the cat-and-mouse game of finding the killer dragged out through spring.

Finding a bottle of peroxide, he poured it over his exposed wound. The bubbling of the fluid in the meaty gash combined with the excruciating pain to reassure him the cleaning was working. Taking a clean kitchen sponge, he scrubbed the inner portion of the wound which still had red dirt from the canyon floor where he had fallen, then poured more peroxide over the inflamed tissue to get out any of the small pieces of the sponge that might adhere to the silvery wound. He pinched the two separated skin flaps together, used Super Glue to close them, then followed up with duct tape for good measure. The final step was to wrap the arm in a clean pink towel left over from a long-ago ex, then create a makeshift sling from an old flour sack.

Not bad, he thought as his mind switched gear back to the great turquoise stone, jumping over the fact that he needed to leave town soon.

The rock's the key. What am I missing? The kid! It has to be that skinny Navajo kid. He had a #35 stone and told me where he found it.

The President realized the most likely answer as to who had tracked him down was the Navajo silversmith who had been his lead to finding the #35 mine in the first place. It had to be him or someone he had talked to. The President had only seen one other stone from this particular deposit, and that was on this skinny Navajo's wrist at the Santa Fe Winter Indian Market. He doubted there were many who could have known the significance of the gem. It took the best to pick it out on the kid's arm in the sea of people crowding the Santa Fe Convention Center.

That kid was now in the crosshairs of one pissed-off ex-Marine. If he was involved, he better have some good answers. If he tried to cover up the truth, the President would know and make him pay dearly.

The President grabbed his cash, a few clothes, and exited his house. He would not come back, not until he figured out who was trying to kill him.

❋ ❋ ❋ ❋

"Hey President, what's with the sling? You get in a fight?"

"No, nothing like that, Leroy. Just fell, that's all, no big deal." The President hoped Leroy didn't smell his morning whiskey breath and ask more questions.

"So what brings you around? Got some work for old Leroy? Been a tough winter around here, not enough jewelry being sold these days. Most of you stone men seem to be hurting. Damn Indonesian fakes are putting the hurt on my local smiths too. Just you big boys who handle the great stones still making a decent living these days."

"Well today is your lucky day, Leroy. I'm still doing business and I got buyers. How long we known each other?"

"Oh, must be going on 30 years, I 'spect. Why you asking, you in trouble with law or something?"

Leroy seemed to suspect something was up. He wasn't buying the falling injury. He probably could see the faint tinge of blood seeping through the President's worn cloth sling.

"Not really trouble, at least not yet, but I got a secret I'll share with you if you can keep it on the QT." The President picked his words carefully. "I'll make it worth the effort, but it's got to be 100% confidential."

"You know my god-given name is Lee Roy Lancaster. Even my own wife don't know Leroy isn't one word, it's Lee Roy, and we've been married nearly 40 years. So what's the big secret?" Leroy's eyes were bugging out.

The President figured Leroy understood that the President was about to make him money, which he needed badly. Reaching into his bulging front pocket with his left hand, the President pulled out the heavy silver/turquoise chunk and tossed it onto what used to be a nice tiger-striped oak table, its golden luster stripped away by Gallup's harsh winter weather. The egg-shaped nugget bounded along the tabletop producing a clicking noise, its silver inclusions causing it to wobble until it found Leroy's leathery hand. The President smiled as he watched the stonecutter's face turn to amazement. They both could tell by the sound alone that this was a great raw turquoise nugget.

Hands that had handled thousands of raw stones gingerly examined the rock. Even the way it rolled on the desk was unique. It had a slight coating on it. Leroy brought it close to his face for a better look. "Interesting rock you got here. Very interesting. Looks like a high-grade weird #8, but it's got too much silver matrix. Whatever it is, it's a damn nice stone. You want me to cut this for you? Should be able to get at least three real nice-size cabs. So what is this, new mine?"

Leroy was excited and he was also fishing. He may have made his living polishing stones but a new great mine that he might get into on the ground floor was a tantalizing proposition for a great stone cutter like Leroy. Information like that was a valuable commodity in Gallup and he knew it.

So did the President.

"Let's just say it's not widely known at this point. I can't talk about it just yet," the President deflected. "You understand, that's why I need your secrecy. I trust you, but I realize a man has bills so I want this kept private, very private. I'll pay your usual lapidary fee plus you can cut off 5 carats and keep that as payment for our secret, but you gotta promise. No room for a loose mouth, otherwise I walk out and no hard feelings."

The President knew Leroy would jump at the opportunity. If Leroy surprised him and didn't want the job, he might have to try other means to get his cooperation. He would hate to do that to an old friend, but #35 was the find of a lifetime and he had someone dangerous on his trail already and he couldn't wait to secure the fortune that would see him through the rest of his days. He needed Leroy's expertise and hoped he could count on the stone cutter keeping his mouth shut.

"No problem. I'll get working on this puppy and have it lickety-split. Come back in the morning and she will be all ready. Mum's the word," Leroy assured. "You want to get one of the cabs mounted in a nice gold bracelet, got a first-class silversmith in Tohatchi who could do a bang-up job with this stuff. Good with gold or silver. He would love to work with a stone of this quality. He's fast, too, turn it right around."

"No, Leroy, I just want it cut for now. I'll see you in the morning. No more questions. I'll be back early, say 8am."

Leroy shook his head eagerly in agreement and then focused back on the rock, sizing up how he would cut it into four pieces.

Heading for the ramshackle door, the President stopped and swiveled back on his heels. He warned his old compadre, "I'm counting on you and I'm sure you understand how serious I am when it comes to my stones. Especially this stone, Leroy."

"Sure, keep my effing mouth shut," Leroy agreed.

The President's glare told the story. Leroy gulped and made a half-hearted smile. He understood.

CHAPTER 3

TOUGH AS NAILS

The President was convinced whoever had shot him would not be satisfied with a flesh wound. He wanted something, probably the mine itself, and the President stood in his way.

Figuring out who this someone was, was a priority. His best guess was it started with that kid in Santa Fe who had turned him on to the #35 stone and the location where he might find more. The kid had given him specific directions and it must have been he who had ratted him out. The kid seemed like a decent person at the time, but he was the most likely suspect for now. The President was pissed at himself for not getting better information. He was Bear Clan, that much he could remember, and was a student in college. Was it in Arizona? New Mexico?

It seemed like he had said he was off on break and making some extra Christmas money at Winter Indian Market selling some of his jewelry. The kid had written his name down and some other facts, but they were back in the President's house somewhere and he couldn't take a chance of going back. He was pissed he hadn't remembered to look for the paper this morning. Once he had decided he was in peril, he'd left the house immediately and wouldn't be back anytime soon.

Luckily, the President had a place to hide while he waited for his stone to be cut, a place where he stashed more money and most importantly, his Glock. It was at his on-again, off-again girlfriend's house. The President needed some time to heal and he could use a woman's company.

Meanwhile he was wracking his brain. The kid's name was something like Mellowhorn. It would come and when it did, someone was going to have to answer some questions. He wouldn't be shot at again.

✣ ✣ ✣ ✣

Leroy was one of the best stonecutters and polishers in the Southwest. He had worked for most of the stone men and was respected by all. He knew the President was not a man to double cross. Leroy wasn't about to ask questions, like why the President had been drinking in the morning? Or why his stone appeared to have blood on it? The President's eyes had said it all: do your job, keep your mouth shut, and don't ask questions.

There was no stone Leroy hadn't seen in the 40 years he'd been doing this, including some of the finest nuggets ever found. But he had never come up against a beast like the one he was trying to cut into three large cabs now.

His first diamond blade broke after just a few minutes of work. The second one lasted halfway through the stone-cutting process. Finally, on the third blade he managed to turn the stone into three large pieces.

It took him a fourth blade to cleave a small four-carat stone off one of the best portions of the largest slab, as his reward. The President didn't tell him how to cut his stone, just to take five carats in payment. He took closer to four, but they were the best. Then he began the laborious process of making them into highly polished cabochons. It would take him into the night.

CHAPTER 4

FEBRUARY 8, NOSE FOR TROUBLE

Giving Leroy the stone would turn out to be a big mistake for the President, one which would involve numerous lives. The newly found #35 was becoming more like #13, an unlucky number for one of the stone men.

However, the President didn't realize this as he drove to the north side of Gallup to hide out at his girlfriend's house. Patsy Clever rented a small, white-washed house just behind the Flame of Fire Ministries. The President liked its location. It was close to God and Blake's Lotaburger. He didn't go to church but eating a green chile cheeseburger on Sunday made him feel as if he did. It never disappointed. The President didn't want to take a chance that the assassin would see his truck so he hid it a block away at a fellow stone man's house that was gone for the month of February, scouting a mine in Australia.

Patsy hid her key behind a ceramic duck whose faded color made it appear more like an albino then the proud mallard it once was.

Once inside the house and finding Pasty not home, he finally relaxed, the first time he allowed himself this luxury since his near-death experience. The night before he had slept in fits from pain and anxiety. He retrieved his Glock and money from his knapsack stashed in the back of Patsy's utility closet with some of his clothes. The gun was always loaded but he checked the cylinder anyway. The solid black grip in his hand made the President feel at ease. Falling onto Patsy's bed, the faint smell of salty sheets acted like a sleeping pill along with the earlier shots of Jack. The President conked out. He slept for two hours until he heard the door rattle, which jerked him into instant alertness. He grabbed the gun and leapt up.

Patsy, who wasn't expecting any company, especially not her on-again, off-again boyfriend of the last 10 years, was also startled and let out a scream upon seeing him pointing his cocked Glock at her face.

"Shhheee, what you screaming about? It's me, goddamnit, you're going to get the cops on us."

"Put that gun away, JFK. You know I hate guns and sure don't like one pointed at me. What the hell are you doing at my home and not calling ahead to tell me you're on your way? This is not your home. You may have made a few payments but that doesn't give you any right to barge in and point a gun at me!"

"Now, now, PC. I'm sorry, but I got myself into a little jam and you're the only one I could turn to." The President tapped his gun on the large bandage around his bicep so she could see he was wounded, the red coloration seeping through the muslin cloth and now soiling the flour-sack sling.

"Oh my god, what happened to you? Have you been to the doctor?"

"Here's the deal and don't freak out, but I got shot."

"Shot! What—"

"Just please be quiet, my love, and listen." He then proceeded to recount why he hadn't been around much in the last two months, then explained in detail his last 24 hours starting with the great rock he'd found and that someone was tracking him and how he was afraid and that's why he went to her place. She was the only person he trusted, plus he was worried whoever was after him might come looking for her too and he wanted to give her a heads-up.

"If you're frightened, then I'm really scared. What if that guy figures out I'm your girlfriend, or kind of girlfriend," PC reasoned, looking for additional recognition of their relationship.

None was forthcoming.

"Listen, whether I'm here or not they will start asking around sooner or later. Whoever this guy or guys are they must know something about me to be able to track me in the desert. I figure we both better high-tail it out of Gallup first thing in the morning. I've got to find out how they found me and why they shot me. I also need time to heal. I'll collect my turquoise cabs that I left for cutting at Leroy's and we can go to a hideout I have, then head up to Toadlena. That's Bear Clan country and I can see if we can't find that kid. He's the key to why my arm's in a sling. I find him, I find the guy who shot me. I doubt seriously it was the kid but he's involved somehow."

The trembling PC fell into the President's chest and good arm. He knew Patsy had a weakness for him and for the excitement he brought into her humdrum life as a substitute schoolteacher barely making ends meet. He held her as tight as he could and reassured her, "I got a nose for trouble, PC, and we aren't there yet. I'll let you know when to worry, I promise. Meanwhile, this little nugget could change everything for both of us." PC started to sob and there was no consoling her.

CHAPTER 5

FEBRUARY 9, PACKING HEAT

As soon as the sun's filtered light seeped through the crack in PC's window shades, she was wide awake. Sleep had been difficult. Nothing physical had occurred, which was fine as they were too emotionally spent.

PC had cleaned the wound on JFK's arm and redressed it with a clean bandage. It was looking like it might heal just fine. A few more days would tell for sure if it was going to get infected. The bloodied flour-sack sling was replaced with a clean bed sheet ripped into segments. No need to go to a medical store for a professional sling and raise suspicion.

For PC, the night had been filled with suspicious noises. She almost woke JFK up to make him leave her house, then considered sneaking over to the ministry building across the lot herself, a place she figured would be safe. But calm reasoning overrode her emotional urges, so instead she rolled around for a few hours before succumbing to exhaustion.

The first order of business was brewing a strong pot of coffee and making plans for their escape. She had packed a bag hastily last night, not taking too much from the closet. If anyone was to break in, she didn't want to let on that she was gone. Having no pets and working only part time as a substitute teacher meant she had no commitments and tried to look at the adventure with JFK as just that, an adventure, not running from a unknown killer. It would be time with a man she cared about even though he couldn't commit. He was 24 years older than she was and they had been involved, or semi-involved, for 10 years now.

It was hard to be with a man who put rocks above love, new finds ahead of proven friendship, and for whom beauty came in only one color, blue. But she could live with those idiosyncrasies as long as she had equal footing when it came time to the important decisions. Maybe this was one of those times. He had come to her and wanted her to leave with him. Perhaps he loved her after all? Deep down she didn't want to think it was because he might want to tie up any loose ends before leaving town, or didn't trust her to keep her mouth shut if somebody came looking for him, but she realized this was a distinct possibility.

JFK had the eggs sizzling and coffee brewing as PC put on her makeup, adding additional base to help conceal newfound lines under her eyes. Looking in the mirror, the image was of an attractive woman, not bad for turning 40 in two weeks. She wondered if the President even knew the monumental birthday was almost here. Probably not.

"So, what's the plan? A girl's got to have some planning in her life," she asked, putting on the brightest front she could in front of him, even though she was terrified of the unfolding events.

He put his arm around her. "Baby, you need to get packed and ready to go as we need to hit the road by 9am. We're going to go hide out for a week, just us. I'll stop at Walmart and get some provisions and ammo. Then we'll head for my safe house. I need to let this arm heal up before I go after a killer."

Hearing "ammo" and "killer" brought the reality of the situation into perspective for Patsy. "What kind of ammo? Don't you already have some?"

"Honey, I'm sorry to do this shit to you, but I need to be ready. Gotta take care of us both. A Marine is always prepared. When and if trouble finds us, I can't risk being shorthanded in the ammo department. I'll let you know when to be worried, for now just get packed up. Make sure you've got warm clothes, nothing fancy. Why don't you get a cartoon of cigarettes, a six pack of Corona, and fill up your car. I'll get my supplies and I want them sooner rather than later, capiche?

"Huh?"

"Get ready. I'll be back in an hour. Here's $200. That should take care of it."

❋ ❋ ❋ ❋

The President did love Patsy in his own way, but her last name Clever did not always live up to the billing, he thought impatiently. This morning required a clear, quick mind, something Patsy didn't have often enough. Well, at least she was willing to drop everything and come away with him.

Walmart was on Maloney Avenue, just two minutes from PC's house. It was nearly empty at 7:30am, which is what the President wanted. He needed ammo for the Glock, duct tape, flashlight, serrated knife, and large garbage bags.

He didn't tell PC about the entire shopping list, afraid he would horrify her. He realized what he was buying was a recipe for a killing spree and if his bill was discovered it would be strong superficial evidence.

He paid cash and wore sunglasses and his beat-up cowboy hat. It was all the disguise he could muster. The sling would probably be remembered but it was nothing he could help.

Securing five cases of ammunition felt reassuring. He realized if it came down to a major shootout, he was probably fucked anyway, but somehow it still eased his mind. At close range he was deadly. From a distance, the rifle marksman would always win.

PC was ready to go when JFK returned. His plan was to bring her car along as a getaway vehicle just in case he needed to ditch his truck.

The President rounded up his own clothes at PC's, organized his gear under a blanket, and headed over to Leroy's with PC following behind. The Glock was now housed safely in its shoulder harness and a case of bullets was packed in his pocket. The President wouldn't be going anywhere unless he was packing.

He drove to Leroy's shop, PC following behind. She waited in her car when he went in to finish his business.

CHAPTER 6

WOW!

Leroy had just put the finishing touches on the three large cabs of unidentified high-grade turquoise. The gem quality of the stones impressed the man who knew his way around a rock. They had a hardness not seen in other turquoise, a dense silver matrix, and robin's egg blue encapsulation. The silver/turquoise was the densest he had ever cut. The silver matrix alone made the piece valuable. He marveled at how ambient light caused the silver to refract the light in such a way that that it resembled a diamond, not turquoise.

The cab Leroy saved for himself, while small, had such a fine matrix he couldn't help commenting, "Wow!" as he fingered it again this morning. Knowing the gem was his to keep or sell was an exciting proposition in lean economic times.

The President quickly strode into Leroy's back room.

Leroy was startled by the President's sudden appearance and hid the stone awkwardly behind his back.

"What you got there, Leroy? One of my stones? Let's see it. From your 'wow,' sounds to me like we got a winner."

Leroy had hoped to show this cab last, not wanting the President to focus in on what he now considered his, understanding how Gollum's precious ring obsession in the *Lord of the Rings* must have started.

The President stared. "Shit, that's better than I even imagined. Being so small, I'm assuming this was what you cleaved for yourself? Hope you didn't take the best piece?"

Leroy gazed downward, probably giving the President the answer to his question even though he said nothing.

"OK," commanded the President. "So where are my cabs? I've seen what you did for yourself, let's see my beauties."

Leroy opened a brown leather pouch that had been lying next to his lapidary machinery and poured three highly polished gemstones into the President's oversized hand.

The President's pupils dilated and an unabashed smile came over his face. "Now that's what I'm talking about, amazing! You are the best in business, no doubt about that." The President methodically eyed each stone with a loupe, touching each with his finger and licking the surface to see how the color changed.

After five minutes of close examination, the President looked over at Leroy and proclaimed in his usual deep, booming voice, "Good job, very nice indeed. I did notice however that the piece you cleaved for your payment was the absolute best part of my rock, wasn't it?"

Leroy broke into a sweat. The President had a reputation as fair but tough, and Leroy wasn't exactly sure which side of the fence he was on at that moment.

"Yeah, I would agree, it was a premium piece of stone, but you didn't say where I could take it from and that piece happened to be where it wouldn't affect the other cabs so I decided that was how I would cut it." Leroy licked his lips as he waited for a response, one he was afraid would be spontaneous and possibly violent.

"Well, can't blame you, I guess. Would have done the same thing myself. Here's the deal, Leroy. If you decide to get rid of the cab, let me know and I'll purchase it from you for a fair amount. Don't just go and sell it. Understand?"

"Sure, no problem, you're the man," Leroy assured, his shoulders relaxing as he wiped his head with his grease-stained long sleeve shirt. "What you figure it's worth, if you was going to buy it from me, being it's so good and all?"

"It's $500 a carat in my top-end market as I see it. I'd give you $400 a carat, which is the best you'll see anywhere, I can assure you."

Leroy knew this was true as the highest he had ever heard of any turquoise selling for was $350 a carat for some great Lander turquoise. "OK, Mr. President, I want to keep it for now, but when I'm ready I'll sell it to you. It's four carats not five, just so you know."

The President leaned over and grinned, showing all his front teeth. "I know, Leroy, why do you think I didn't knock your block off? You were smart to take the best cleavage and smarter not to get too greedy. Hogs get fat, pigs get slaughtered. Remember, I get first right of refusal."

He paid Leroy's lapidary bill in cash and headed outside where PC was waiting, slouching in her driver's seat.

As Leroy watched, the President got into his pickup, gunned the engine and flew off, tires spinning and PC trying to keep up.

Leroy plopped down into an overstuffed chair, his legs shaky. He'd been smart. He wondered if he could stay that way.

CHAPTER 7

RAISING CAPITAL

The President knew two things for sure: he was one step ahead of a killer and he needed to raise some capital. His best buyer for great turquoise nuggets was in Japan. Selling one of the cabochons to his Japanese Whale only required two iPhone photos and a sales pitch text of three words: "The best ever!" Mr. Hamoshomi, or Ham as the stone men coined him, was a glutton for anything blue. He was delighted and more than willing to pay the $500 a carat.

The President knew he could sell all three cabs if he wanted, but figured if the vein was small, then $500 a carat might actually be below what the market would bear. He had seen it once before with the Lander mine. Found in 1973 in Lander County, Nevada, it only produced 100 pounds of turquoise. It was the best ever found till #35 was discovered two days ago. The President had possessed 10 pounds of Lander turquoise and sold it too cheap. He wouldn't repeat that mistake. He would hedge his bet until he could get back to look for more signs of turquoise.

He kept two cabochons for himself, separating out the smallest cab, which still consisted of numerous carats. He wrapped the cab in one of his clean bandages and dropped it in a FedEx box on his way out of town. In one day the money would be wired safely into his account.

He would head to Grey's Quarry to mend. The small quarry had been shut down for years and was 25 miles out of town, a place even the locals didn't know about. The President used the grounds to blow up large rock formations. The owner was a friend who lived in Grants and didn't mind if he used the place. The President had a key to the small metal shed, which also had running water and a john.

He kept thinking about the kid, the one who had possessed the only other known example of #35. A 20ish Navajo who was a part-time silversmith, the kid had been selling a small group of bracelets at Winter Market. They were all well executed in a modern design, but there was nothing particularly unusual about the stones except for the one on his wrist. That personal bracelet was not for sale. The kid had explained it was his first bracelet that he had made and it had sentimental attachment. The stone was amazing, from the soon-to-be-#35. The kid's stone was just as good as what the President had just sold Ham, but very small, maybe three carats. That bracelet was not for sale, but the location where he had found the stone was.

The President had paid $100 dollars for a map to the area, promising that the kid would receive an additional $100 finder's fee if the President found a nugget there himself. The President tore in half a $100 bill and placed it on the kid's show table next to the bracelets for sale, promising, "You get me to that place you found your stone and I'll bring you the other half as a finder's fee." The kid had given his number and address, which the President had stuffed into some drawer at his house. What he did remember clearly was the kid's story about finding the mine.

It went like this: during his senior year in high school, the kid drove his great aunt to Crownpoint to sell a rug. He had time to kill while the auction took place, so he drove east on County Road 48 till it bent back south. There was an old sheep pen at that junction next to a low-riding white mesa. The pen was the kind that his ancestors made, pushed up against a cliff wall.

Once at the pen, he parked and walked north until there was a tall south-facing rock wall that had a line of petroglyphs with an unusual number of circle motifs. A small crack in the earth at the east end of the ruin was an escape hatch to the top of the mesa. There was a hole that was obscured by boulders but once through the boulders it was easy to climb to the top. Once on top he headed east to a series of slot canyons. It was in the first slot canyon next to a large funny-shaped dead juniper that he had found the nugget. The kid didn't know if there were many more stones but figured there must be, as he had seen some old Nasazi turquoise beads with the same-looking stone at the fringe of an anthill as he ate lunch. He had left these beads alone, not wanting to disturb the Nasazi sprits.

The President had dedicated the next few months to finding this stone cache. Luckily it had been a dry winter with minimal snow coverage. Finding the ancient sheep camp had been easy enough. He had spent his first half day looking through ant hills there, uncovering a single bead the size of a baby aspirin which appeared to be #35. He searched more ant hills along an Anasazi ruin and found two more beads.

Those beads propelled him all winter. He knew there had to be turquoise. On and off, he kept searching, employing a methodical reconnaissance with a zigzag approach up and down the endless slot canyons that make up a good part of the eastern Navajo Reservation. He searched near sunset to avoid being seen. Also, the grazing light was good for spotting glints of metal which was the matrix of this turquoise cache.

Bennie Begay, an elderly Navajo who owned the property, had stopped the President the first week of his search. Bennie politely but firmly told him this was his land and to get off. The President again plied money, this time in the form of a nice jacula necklace which he wore around his neck. It had deep-blue gemstones worn smooth from use, and was painful to give away since he had worn it for so many years, but finding #35 had been worth the cost. He told Bennie he was a fossil hunter, promising if he found anything of value he would give him another necklace. Bennie no doubt thought the *bilagaana* was crazy and wished him luck, believing it was highly unlikely he'd find fossils and he appeared happy just to have a great necklace he could pawn if he ever needed to.

What the President didn't know was that Bennie had his own jacula, made entirely of #35 nuggets he had found tending sheep as a kid. It was on his neck as he talked to the *bilagaana*, hidden under two layers of coats.

Now, the President wracked his brain to remember any other encounters that could have gotten him fingered, but he figured it came down to only Bennie Begay or the kid. He had seen a few trucks and cars each time he drove in the area, but they appeared to be employee vehicles heading to or from the CXI mine, a lower-grade turquoise mine just outside Begay's property on private land. Never did he see any vehicle on Begay's land other than Begay's truck.

He finally had cracked the code of the stones when he started looking for prehistoric paths that would lead back to the ancient ones' living quarters, which now were rubble ruins. The President figured that the turquoise cache must be away from the ceremonial picture wall and closer to the village. He discovered a grouping of 20 Anasazi structures, which had been reduced to one-foot raised piles of well-organized flat rocks. Once the home base was discovered it was only a matter of making ever larger circles outward till he finally found what he was looking for, turquoise-laced rocks. It still didn't add up.

Two and a half months of looking with only one human encounter, then the attempt to kill him? He hid his truck each time near a slot canyon before he searched the area, and took every precaution to avoid being seen and never heard vehicle noise other than Begay's truck. Yet the day he finds the rock, the day he blurts out a sound, he gets shot. He must have been followed. That's all he could figure. Maybe the kid wasn't involved. Maybe it was more sinister than he imagined.

CHAPTER 8

BILAGAANAS ABOUND

Bennie Begay had spent many of his 78 years away from his homeland. He was born to the Bitter Water Clan. His current home was in the same hogan in which he had been born. His mother was a weaver, as was her mother, and her mother's mother before her, but weaving stopped with Bennie. He was an only child and his mom died when he was 17. He joined the Navy, fought in Korea, and came back to the US with training in heavy machinery. He worked in California for 25 years for the state. He didn't mind the work and it paid well, but ultimately he couldn't hack city life and came back home.

He now lived comfortably on a small retirement fund, social security, and a minor allotment. Begay farmed, took care of his animals, and earned extra income from chopping juniper wood when he needed it from his large landholding. He had one son, Ernie, whom he'd fathered with a Mission Indian in California. His son knew nothing of the Navajo Reservation. Bennie hoped this would change someday, so he could see him regularly and teach him about his ancestors and the land that would be his inheritance.

Most days Bennie was content to stay home and tend to his few sheep and chickens. In the summer he raised a modest garden near a seasonal creek. He had few personal possessions and wasn't one to want. He owned a couple of nice old cluster bracelets from the 1940s and two jaculas, the one he'd put together as a kid and the one he'd recently been given by the *bilagaana*. His mother's last rug which was halfway done hadn't been moved in 61 years since her death from a truck rollover, a memorial to her memory and to all his grandmothers who had woven before her. As far as he knew he had no other close relatives other than people in his clan. Bernie loved his log hogan, as meager as it was. The trees near his home were large and impressive; these he never touched except to occasionally give them extra water and fertilizer, unusual by his people's standards. Diné believe if the tree lives in a harsh environment it's meant to, and if it dies then it becomes firewood.

Visitors to Bennie's place were uncommon, especially of the *bilagaana* variety. He had only had two come to his house in the last decade, and both in the last year.

The first *bilagaana* was an odd-sounding man five months ago who had sought him out. The man knew his name without being introduced and offered to lease his land without even making small talk. He promised lots of money. Bernie explained he wasn't interested in leasing his land and having more money wouldn't change his life as much as destroying the land would. It was ancestral property and he had a responsibility to his forefathers. Plus he didn't like the man. The *bilagaana* explained he was interested in some kind of rocks that were adjacent to his property and he was mining them on his land, which touched the Begay property. The man with the funny accent didn't like it when Bernie told him that Mother Earth was not to be scarred with big machines, that if it was deeper than what you could dig up with a hoe, it was too deep.

The man could do what he wanted as long as it wasn't on Diné land, but Bennie had seen the impact of what mankind is capable of with the help of heavy machinery. So: no lease, end of story. The man never returned, but Bennie could hear the large tractors tearing into the earth some 10 miles south of his property. He hoped the visitor would not come back.

Bennie had first thought that the fossil hunter was another one of the mine men, but he wore a Navajo jacula and understood Diné, so Bernie figured him to be a good human, just not very smart about dinosaurs, but harmless. His eyes were kind and he talked straight. Bernie invited him into the house and the man took the time to make small talk and share coffee before asking for permission to use his land. Bernie didn't worry when he saw him walking around day after day for endless hours looking for bones that didn't exist.

The funny-talking man was a different story: his eyes lacked emotion and maybe a coyote spirit was behind the mask. Begay had seen what looked like a coyote spirit in the shape of a man a few times at dusk, mirroring the man with the kind eyes. He was not sure what to make of what he thought he had seen until the evening he heard the gunshots.

Afraid to go out that night, Bennie had checked in the morning and found blood and many human tracks but no trace of what animal the blood had come from. He had not seen the kind-eyed man in the last week and worried what might have become of him.

CHAPTER 9

IT HAPPENED LAST YEAR

The year 2013 saw much change in gallery owner Charles Bloom's world. Bloom's near-death experience at Hidden Canyon made him realize he was a fool not to sanctify his love to such a wonderful and strong person as Rachael Yellowhorse.

In May 2013, in the courtyard of Bloom's Santa Fe art gallery, surrounded by the most important people in their lives, the couple exchanged their vows. Apple trees in bloom and a few of Rachael's old sculptures provided an ideal setting for this event in the life of the longtime bachelor who always had said he would never get married. The guest list was supposed to be no more than 25, but soon ballooned to 40. The small coyote-fenced patio was standing room only. His best friend Brad Shriver acted as Bloom's best man and hosted the after-party drinks and food in his next-door gallery, closing for the day, a rare event for Shriver, who knew how to get the most out of his retail space especially in May.

Rachael was in the last week of her first trimester with their second child and barely showing when they married. The name had been already selected: Samantha Jo Yellowhorse Bloom, after Detective

Samuel Hubbard of the San Francisco Police Department, who also attended the wedding. If not for Hubbard's exceptional detective work in the months prior there would have never been a wedding as there would be no Bloom. Hubbard had tracked down a deranged killer who had set his sights on the entire Bloom family.

The couple had discussed a variety of places for a honeymoon, but money and time were scarce. Rachael had only a few precious months before Indian Market and she was nowhere near finishing her big rug for the summer season. Little Willy, their firstborn, was almost one and didn't care about any rug project. It was decided that Santa Fe as a honeymoon retreat would do nicely, with one caveat: no work allowed. Bloom splurged for a room at the Inn of the Anasazi, one of the best hotels in town. He had recommended the great pueblo-style hotel for years to his clients, but this was the first time he stayed there himself. The bar there had always been one of his favorite places for a margarita. Like its salty agave treats, the hotel did not disappoint. Tasteful, authentic Native American décor and a top-notch staff also made the stay memorable.

Holding hands on the hotel patio, they discussed what life held before them and how much they both had changed together in the last three years. Rachael the non-drinker enjoyed watching Bloom observe the tourists stroll by with his favorite high-octane drink in hand. Since Bloom planned to remember each second of the night, he gave himself a two-drink limit. It was an odd feeling to be in Santa Fe and not worried if tourists would find his gallery and spend money before heading back to Texas. He was relaxed with his soul mate, knowing a second baby was on the way. Bloom's life was in balance and concern with money was not part of the night's equation. It was a fulfilling wedding and a special weekend at the Anasazi. If only life could remain so easy.

The next big event of 2013 was the arrival of Samantha Jo Yellowhorse Bloom right on schedule on December 7. Dr. Carson Riddly was the attending physician, as he had been for Willy. Sammy, as she was already being called, was a healthy six pounds with bright brown eyes, a shock of chocolate hair, and a strong pair of vocal cords.

Dr. Riddly was now the doctor of choice for most Navajo mothers to be. Hastiin Johnson's recommendation to use Dr. Carson as an obstetrician at Willy's smiling ceremony had ensured a full schedule of newborns for the young Doctor Riddly. The added burden had paid off as Carson Riddly had become quite proficient in the art of birthing babies. The once hesitant Riddly realized his true passion was in this discipline and wondered if the erudite Hastiin Johnson had seen something in him that he couldn't recognize himself. Carson had developed such an interest in the field that he had applied to and had been accepted at UNM Medical School to do a three-year residency in ob/gyn. Carson was still dating his Navajo girlfriend Brenda Wildhorse. Their relationship was strong but no engagement ring had been forthcoming. Brenda was hesitant to leave a good job and her close-knit family to follow Carson to Albuquerque, a place he was considering as a long-term stopping point. For his part, Carson wanted to make sure that he was able to juggle a demanding residency before adding the additional responsibility of a significant other. Brenda loved Kayenta and it wasn't clear if she would ever be willing to leave the reservation. Carson decided if in a year's time he and Brenda couldn't stand to be apart from each other then they should get married and not worry about where they ultimately settled down.

Bloom had been impressed that the good doctor had been able to convince himself this would work. Carson obviously didn't understand the significant effect that Diné women had on mere mortals, even four hours away.

CHAPTER 10

FEBRUARY 9, IN SANTA FE

It was this distance phenomenon that currently had Bloom's world out of harmony. It was February 9, 2014, and he was in Santa Fe while his wife and children were back home in Navajoland. Rachael, always the trouper, was taking care of the whole brood by herself and working diligently on her rug for August's Indian Market.

All had been calm in Bloom's life until a week ago. A broken pipe beneath the bathroom floor of his gallery had caused havoc and hastened his return to Canyon Road. Bloom figured a decent plumber could replace the pipe, he could get the red-brick flooring repaired, and he could be back home in a week and meanwhile maybe make a sale or two while he was in Santa Fe.

Charles Bloom had never been a fan of Santa Fe's winter, but a short break from the rez had seemed a nice diversion from Sammy's poorly formed sleep habits. Now that he'd been here a week, the repairs were pretty much done and he was feeling the isolation of not being with his family and yet Santa Fe also had a hold on him.

As he struggled to break the layer of ice that had formed overnight on his gallery's brick entrance, Bloom remembered Rachael suggesting last summer, "Wouldn't it be nice to have one of those heated snow mats instead of shoveling snow? Big Jo's is having a sale on them, 50% off!" He had never made it down to Siler Road that August day of his wife's insightful observation. Summer was a time when money flowed and snow mats were cheap. It was now winter and money was tight and self-cleaning porches only a dream. In the future he would listen closer to his wife's sage advice. Rachael was right as usual, which was evident by his stiff lower back. He was missing their warm bed and her supple body.

Bloom loved his quaint Canyon Road with art connoisseurs strolling by providing the essential nourishment: the retail sale. The "city different" had been his home for most of his adult life. Yet something had changed. An adjustment in equilibrium was taking place. No doubt having a wife and two children was part of the formula, but somehow inexplicably the rez itself had become meaningful to his existence. It had only been seven days since he last saw his Two Grey

Hills with their ever-changing hues and the tip of Shiprock, his beacon of home. Sculpture on every Santa Fe corner, while compelling, could not compete with Mother Nature's geological splendor, which surrounded his rez home in Toadlena.

He looked around his gallery, thinking he should pack up and head down I-25 toward Albuquerque, then west to Navajoland. At the same time, he hesitated, needing some kind of battery recharge he couldn't quite understand. The hustle and bustle of Santa Fe's population of 70,000 seemed almost deafening compared to the isolation of the rez. Where did he belong?

Bloom's gallery was on cruise control. His sole employee, Dr. J, knew the ropes, having worked at the gallery for several years, many of those months without the help of the boss, and ran it just fine. With minimal tourist traffic this time of year, there was no real need for Bloom to stay. Even Bloom knew that his presence was not needed, more a distraction to his employee. He would check his email one more time.

And then, just as he decided it was time indeed to leave, otherworldly forces intervened. An email followed by a phone call sealed his fate: a special emergency meeting of the Indian Arts and Crafts Association was being mounted in Santa Fe tomorrow morning, February 10th, at the behest of the antifraud art unit of the FBI, and Charles Bloom's presence was requested.

Indian art was Bloom's lifeblood, as it was for many galleries in Santa Fe. His, however, was the only one that specialized in contemporary Native art. The IACA was a trade group important to Bloom and most Southwest dealers of Indian art. Fake turquoise jewelry, knock-off baskets, commercial kachinas, and even pseudo Navajo-style rugs had been problematic for as long as Charles had been in Santa Fe, but the problem was mounting. To stem the flow, the District Attorney and the Feds had been cracking down on galleries that sold fake Indian goods to unsuspecting tourists. Now the FBI was reaching out directly to those that were on the front lines and apparently Bloom was included in that battle plan, or so it seemed.

❋ ❋ ❋ ❋

An attractive woman pushing 40 chaired the morning's IACA meeting. FBI agent Shirley Simplton. Her brass-colored name tag made Charles smile. With all those "s" sounds, he thought of his own Sammy, wondering when he would see her first smile. Hopefully it wouldn't be directed toward Hastiin Johnson, as Charles was not prepared for another huge party at Johnson's behest.

Today's meeting participants came in all colors and descriptions. Many were in their 50s and 60s, laden in turquoise and silver. Some wore cowboy hats. All had serious looks on their faces. Bloom recognized a few of them, mostly local characters he would bump into at Indian Market or at the Shed for green chile corn chowder, but the majority were unknown entities. These were not his painting-dealer colleagues but rougher in appearance, true New Mexicans.

The bitch fest in the room began immediately. Bloom sat back and listened. Officer Simplton let them vent. There were numerous complaints identifying dealers on the Plaza as the problem. The "50% off" signs, "going out of business" banners every three months, the increase in Middle Eastern-owned shops, and of course prevalent Native-style jewelry made all over the globe were hot topics that never seemed to find a consensus as far as a solution. The individuals that advertised monthly teasers for the unsuspecting tourist of course were not members of IACA but rather never-ending thorns in the sides of the hard-working merchants who loved authentic Indian art and did belong to the IACA.

There was no doubt a few in the audience might risk the chance to pass off fakes if the opportunity afforded itself, but lately the costs in terms of fines and even jail had stopped most of the fringe element from being tempted.

Finally Officer Simplton took charge. She was an impressive figure. A dishwater blond who stood just five-foot-two, she had an athletic build and stunning features which were highlighted by her tight business attire. Bloom's pupils couldn't help but dilate when she stood up, her tight belt accentuating her impressively large breasts. He hadn't expected any FBI agent to be a female, much less as attractive as Shirley Simplton. He tried to focus on the message she was presenting with her baritone voice, and not her striking profile.

"OK, settle down. You all have had a chance to air your dirty laundry and all of it is legitimate but that's not why I'm here. My name is

Officer Simplton, but don't let the name fool you." She smiled then winked, seemingly at Bloom's corner of the room. He blushed for no good reason.

"I need to ask you all to help me with a project the Bureau is working on. I'm passing around four bracelets, numbered one through four, and I would like each of you to examine them closely and make notes on the provided paper. Please do not consult with each other. Provide a tribal attribution for the maker and any other interesting observations you might make as far as the turquoise and workmanship."

Bloom, who sold paintings, sculpture, and rugs, rather than jewelry, didn't have a clue, so he simply wrote "not qualified to offer an educated opinion."

Some 15 minutes later, the bracelets were passed back up front along with about a dozen yellow papers. Simplton quickly tabulated the results, pushed back her chair from her metal desk and stood up, clearing her throat to quiet the crowd.

"OK, here are the results." She made four columns on a 1950s blackboard whose years of usage had left remnant ghost outlines of teachers gone by. "All but two of you who responded thought they were Indian-made. Eight believed they were of Navajo origin, while two thought they were Zuni. One person made the comment that they were fake. Several said they did not know."

She paused for dramatic effect. "Well I'm sorry to inform my esteemed audience, *all* the pieces were fakes. And though they look impressive, they are wholesaling for between $25 and $50 dollars each, a shockingly low price!" A hush went over the audience. As the information seeped in, it soon turned to quiet grumbling.

"You now know why I wanted to meet with you today," said Simplton. "These types of low cost, superior-quality fakes could be devastating to the Indian jewelry market and a real problem for you from the standpoint of the law, not to mention ruinous competition if your fellow dealers start pushing these bracelets as real and undercut the market. So what's the rationale behind most of you dealers who should be in the know, thinking they were really Indian-made?"

Numerous hands went up. The majority mentioned the great turquoise and excellent craftsmanship. The turquoise seemed to be the kicker. Fakes just didn't have quality turquoise and never from Southwestern mines. The stamping was handmade, as were the bezels, all precision craftsmanship. They appeared to be of sterling silver. Many believed that if they had been given time or if they had been offered the pieces at such low prices, they might have come to a different conclusion. They also complained that they weren't given magnifying loupes for a closer inspection.

"You are correct, these pieces are made of very good turquoise. In fact, it appears to our experts who have examined these fakes, that the turquoise is indeed from Nevada, New Mexico, or Arizona. They are natural material. No one has yet to explain how the forgers, who one would assume are located outside the US, could be selling it cheap enough to get it back to the States and make a profit, especially since they are of sterling silver and handmade. They are not using any plastic filler, folks. This is real, natural turquoise, which all of you can appreciate. This is why we believe the bracelets are being made locally, as unlikely as that may seem, even though we are 99% sure they are not Native made." Simplton had her audience's attention.

"Folks, this is the biggest issue we have had in 75 years since mandating laws to stop fakes in Native jewelry. And it's up to you on the front lines to help us by being educated as to what's going on in *your* market. Cheap fakes are about to hit the market and we need you as the go-betweens to help us stop and incarcerate these forgers that are trying to take food out of your and your artists' mouths."

CHAPTER 11

WE NEED YOU!

Simplton pontificated for 30 additional minutes, offering more details as to why they were so sure the pieces were fakes and not Native-made. She could tell many in the audience couldn't recognize the slight differences that made the bracelets forgeries and probably never would.

Then she switched gears, giving the audience the background on how the FBI had obtained the bracelets. "The four bracelets I handed out were intercepted by chance two weeks ago. A pickup truck with New Mexico plates skidded on black ice while coming up La Bajada hill to Santa Fe. The truck flipped, killing the Navajo driver, and spilling bracelets along northbound I-25. We don't know how many bracelets were in the load, as at least two cars stopped and stole bracelets. I might add that these individuals did not help the mortally injured driver. An eyewitness to the scene that did stay around to help, identified two separate cars as stopping, the drivers saying something to the effect of, 'You don't need my help, I guess,' and then appearing to help themselves to a handful of jewelry. The pilfered bracelets came to the attention of the local police. An estimate of value on the pieces was needed in order to file charges against the jewelry thieves. The bracelets were taken to one Lieutenant Poh, who also happens to be a San Ildefonso Indian and a well-respected silversmith. He noticed something unusual with regards to the stamp work and notified the FBI."

Simplton rolled her sleeves up. "We believe the initial load consisted of an estimated 200 bracelets in four distinct styles, on the surface all appearing to be Navajo made. They were in four separate boxes. Approximately 20 bracelets from two of the boxes were taken, but we're still investigating, looking for other eyewitnesses or someone to come forward."

She paused and took a breath. "The Navajo driver who was killed was named Marshall Hanson. He was of the Bitter Water Clan. His family resided near Toadlena, New Mexico. His immediate family was interviewed. They have no knowledge of the jewelry. They claim to be weavers and can't understand why Marshall would be involved in Indian jewelry. The deceased Navajo was not a silversmith, but appears to have been a courier. He did driving for various galleries and jobbers between Santa Fe and Phoenix. He was in trouble with the law off and on, but for the last year had no problems."

She continued, "Since the discovery of the cache two weeks ago, a few similar bracelets have started to pop up across the reservation. All have come from Navajo sources and the two that have been tracked down deny they are not real. The sellers profess these to be Navajo-made using a cheap local source of turquoise but won't disclose its whereabouts. None of them could explain why the pieces looked so similar, but because they said they made them, no charges have been brought, at least not yet. We don't believe these to be pieces taken from the accident scene at this point."

Even though Simplton was a guest at the IACA meeting, she'd taken it over with her news and authoritative manner. "Going forward, those of you here today *must* make detailed notes on anyone selling jewelry that resembles the pieces I passed around today. If you do not and it comes to our attention, you face abetting a felony and risk federal prosecution. This is serious stuff, folks, and we intend to nip it in the bud."

Simplton had Bloom's full attention now, her figure no longer as captivating.

She distributed catalogs filled with high-resolution images of the four styles of bracelets and a few other suspected pieces. "FBI" was inscribed in bold red letters on the front cover. This was not the type of advertising one would want displayed on the front counter of one's Indian arts store. Simplton allowed as how one potential source was Thailand as that country had a long history of fake Indian jewelry, but because the pieces were of such high quality it was hard to imagine that they could be manufactured there with quality Southwestern turquoise, shipped back to the States, and wholesale for $25 to $30 apiece, especially in light of them being sterling silver. A Navajo example of similar quality would wholesale at $125 to $150.

The mood of the crowd was downtrodden as the meeting adjourned, all feeling defeated against the battering ram of life in the American Indian art trade. Many in the audience complained that those that didn't belong to IACA were the individuals that needed to be threatened, not honest dealers that played by the rules. If the cold, icy winter with poor retail sales wasn't enough pain, now there were great cheap fakes flooding the market, and if they screwed up and bought any, then they faced stiff fines or possibly prison while those that didn't play by the rules would make it that much harder to compete.

Bloom, who didn't deal in jewelry, understood that Navajo rugs might be the next item to be faked at a professional level. And many of his new Navajo relatives were bound to be hurt since jewelry and rugs are the lifeline for the Diné, helping to pay for the essentials of life, like gas, food, and clothes. If the market for Navajo jewelry became threatened then he too was in trouble as was Santa Fe's reputation as a place for quality Native-made art.

As he was leaving the meeting, Simplton grabbed Bloom's arm and pulled him close to her chest. It was an awkward moment, which to Bloom seemed inappropriate.

"Mr. Bloom, not so fast, you and I need to talk," she smiled but didn't loosen her grip, pulling him even closer.

"Sure, how can I help you, Officer Simplton?"

"Call me Shirley." Her strong left hand finally relaxed enough for Bloom to retrieve his arm.

"OK Shirley, how can I be of service?" Bloom eased back a bit, feeling uncomfortably close.

"You're married to a master weaver from Toadlena, correct? Rachael Yellowhorse?"

"Yes, we're recently married."

Simplton again stepped into Bloom's uncomfortable personal space and lowered her voice to a deep whisper. "I need an inside informant, someone who can travel in both worlds. As far as I can tell, you're the perfect fit. You deal with Native artists, you have a Navajo wife and kids, and the source of fake pieces seems to originate where your wife has lived her entire life. You're respected by your peers and seem to be ethical, a rarity in your profession. So what do you say, want to work for the FBI? We would be working closely together." Simplton stepped back and turned ever so slightly sidewise so as to accentuate her best assets.

Bloom looked around to see who was watching, as suddenly he felt like he was already her informant and for no good reason. "Well, thanks, I guess, but I don't know if I'm cut out to be working with the FBI. I'm an art dealer and quite frankly I'm not sure that working in that capacity would be a very good career move."

"Can I call you Charles?"

"Of course."

"So Charles, don't make a decision on the spot. I know I ambushed you. This isn't the right place to decide or to discuss it. Let's get to know each other and I can fill you in on why it's important to help us stop this criminal activity. If you would, come see me tomorrow. I'll be up at the courthouse, say 9am sharp?"

"Um, I was planning on going back home to Toadlena...."

"I insist, you need to see the bigger picture. You can spare a few minutes before heading out of town. After all, this is FBI business and I am asking you nicely."

"I guess I can delay getting off a bit. Alright, I'll see you at 9."

"Great, then it's a date. And please, don't be late. The FBI has made me a stickler for promptness. You'll find that out about me." She winked, "If you're lucky you might find out a few other things as well. By the way, keep our upcoming meeting to yourself. This includes the little woman."

Bloom's face turned two shades of red and he exited the room quickly, without saying a word. He didn't know whether to be excited or frightened, but was strongly leaning toward the later. Shirley Simplton's name no longer brought a smile to his face. She was trouble and Toadlena seemed far away.

CHAPTER 12

WELCOME TO THE FORCE

That night Bloom decided against mentioning anything to Rachael, for now. He would wait and talk to Officer Simplton in the morning. Maybe there was a good reason not to confide in Rachael. He would heed Shirley's warning and wait to hear her out. Simplton was petite in stature but her demeanor warned "don't screw with me."

It was around 7pm when Bloom and Rachael talked. If they were together at home, they would have gathered for the dinner hour at the kitchen table. It was their together time and both looked forward to hearing about the other's day. The Internet and cell connections in Toadlena were sketchy at best, so no FaceTime for Bloom. Tonight he was just as happy Rachael couldn't see his face. She might be able to detect something was wrong. Rachael was good at sizing up people, especially her husband. Not saying anything about Shirley Simplton and tomorrow's FBI meeting seemed wrong, since he was pretty sure Shirley was hitting on him, either personally or professionally. It was a perplexing position. He was instructed not to say anything by the FBI yet his heart told him it was wrong. For tonight, nothing would be mentioned but small talk. With two small children, there was plenty of that. Bloom was amazed by Rachael.

She never complained even under trying conditions. He was lucky to have her and loved her deeply. The level of angst he had experienced around Shirley Simplton reinforced his commitment to his spouse. Bloom promised Rachael he would head for home the next day.

He would meet with Simplton then quietly escape back to the rez and out of the Feds' grasp. Little did he know that his return to the rez was exactly what Shirley was counting on.

❋ ❋ ❋ ❋

Federal buildings in Santa Fe tend to be unique with their antiquated history and undecipherable floor plans. Their only redeeming quality is they are filled with wonderful artwork, including masterpieces from the WPA period. New Mexico suffered greatly in the 1930s and if not for art commissions most artists would have starved or been forced to give up their professions. The building Simplton was working out of was a throwback to this time. A particularly compelling William Shuster fresco caught Bloom's attention at the entrance. Having never visited the building, he couldn't help but take time to appreciate the masterpiece. The painting was of cubist-shaped men constructing an adobe building. In some parts of New Mexico, that still occurred. By the time he realized he needed to get moving he was late. Bloom finally found Simplton's small office tucked away in the far rear of the building's basement, opening her door at 9:15.

"Late, Bloom. Our meeting was 9am sharp, not 9:15."

Bloom didn't like the sound of her voice, especially since he didn't work for her and at that moment doubted he ever would.

"Take a seat."

The flirting he thought he perceived yesterday had evaporated. It was now all business. Bloom dropped into a rusted metal chair, which reacted with a large creak. A throwback to the sixties, it was just the sort of mainstay chair that could be found in many Navajo hogans he had visited.

Shirley got the point. "We have a serious issue with these bracelets and I didn't expound on how problematic these implications are for the Santa Fe Native arts community. Those fakes are very good, too good, that's the problem. We can't figure out why anyone would make fakes that must be sold at a significant loss on each piece. To do this just to infiltrate the Indian jewelry market makes no financial sense unless there is a bigger goal in mind, much bigger."

"What do you mean? I would think ripping off Native people's livelihoods is goal enough," Charles commented.

"My background with the Bureau is working in the art fraud division. I have been working in this field for close to 20 years. In all that time I have never come across a forger whose goal was to deceive and not make money. These guys don't seem to be out to make a profit and this is what bothers us. It doesn't make sense. The selling of the jewelry seems like a diversion possibly for some other activity. There has to be an alternative reason for wanting to bring down the price of Navajo jewelry. Maybe not just Navajo, but all Native jewelry. But that reason is not clear to us, not yet. The only way to crack this case is to go undercover. And guess what, you're the best man for the job. In fact, the only man for the job." Simplton took dead aim at Bloom's eyes, never flinching.

Bloom felt trapped. He broke out in a sweat in the cold, damp basement office. "You know I'm an art dealer, right? Not a jewelry dealer, not a police officer. I have absolutely no training, zero, hell I don't even know how to use a weapon. Does this seem like the guy you want snooping around looking for some plotters against the Navajo Nation? These guys won't be happy to find some art dealer sticking his nose where it's not supposed to be."

This was when Shirley laid her cards on the table. "I know you're inexperienced in undercover work, but I also have reviewed your biography, and not the one you have on your gallery website but the one the cops keep. You helped solve a string of murders and capture a very smart and dangerous killer in New York City. You handled yourself admirably under severe pressure three years ago, and from what I can tell, you were quite resourceful in a less than ideal situation."

She nodded her head approvingly. "This type of ability whether you appreciate or disregard it, has not gone unnoticed by the FBI. Not only do you have a valuable skill set but it's what else you bring to the table that is irreplaceable. You deal in Indian art and have for more than 20 years. You're married to a Navajo that comes from Toadlena. The one human clue we have was from there. And you're a known entity and trusted on the reservation. All I need you to do is to start an adjunct business along with your contemporary art, dealing in Indian jewelry. This way you can start buying from the locals, who will seek you out. Once the word gets out, we will nail them. The Bureau will provide you capital of up to $50K to buy merchandise, which helps out the local honest economy around Toadlena."

Shirley made clear, "Your job will be to find and purchase the fake jewelry and then give us those leads. Nothing else, no cloak and dagger kind of stuff. Just names and addresses. No one will know but you and the Bureau that you provide us with the information. We will keep you out of any danger."

Bloom struggled with a rebuttal. "That's all well and good but *how* am I supposed to know what's fake and not? I'm not an expert in this field. I wrote that on my little yellow slip you handed out yesterday, remember? You must know my gallery specializes in modern art by contemporary Native artists—specifically, paintings and sculpture. The only traditional art I handle is my wife's rugs and an occasional reproduction petroglyph which is not traditional Navajo."

"I understand all this. So bring your silversmith nephew on board for a few weeks to help legitimize your standing. We understand he is quite a good jeweler and we can pay him a stipend, through you of course. He won't know what's going on. He's just helping you diversify your product line, a normal practice in business. We also have an expert ready to help educate you in traditional Navajo jewelry. Remember I said one person recognized the fakes yesterday? His name is Jake Johnson, goes by Blue. He is an old-school Indian art trader who knows his way around Native jewelry and the reservation. He has a small problem with the IRS, a matter of a pending felony charge for grossly underpaying a decade of taxes. He would like to see these charges obviated and is happy to pitch in for a few weeks. He is quite motivated and at your undivided disposal. We made all the arrangements yesterday."

Bloom's heart sunk. "So you're telling me, not asking for my help? And you want to pair me with a felon who will work with me under duress? Does that sum it up?"

"*Telling* is a strong word. I would say we are strongly requesting your help as we are with Mr. Blue and he's no felon, at least not yet, and don't forget you also get to help your people and get your nephew some serious walking around money."

"And if I decline this request of generosity and choose to avoid getting myself into a world that's maybe too dangerous for an art dealer like myself?"

Shirley sighed. "I will be available at any time to help you. I'm your point man, so to speak. You don't have to worry about getting hurt, unless you don't cooperate, then quite frankly I can't protect you or your family."

"What do you mean, protect us? That sounds like a threat," Charles objected.

"Not a threat, just the reality of the situation. I predict the shit is going to hit the fan on this one and when that does we will throw out a wide, all-encompassing net. Many Navajos will likely go to jail. Names are already being accumulated as persons of interest. I would hate to see yours included or Rachael's, for that matter. That is your wife's name, right? Besides, there can be fringe benefits to assisting the FBI. For instance, you get to work with me." Simplton shot a wicked smile in Bloom's direction.

This was blackmail and borderline sexual harassment, but there were no viable options as far as Bloom could see. He didn't want to go up against the FBI and ultimately he realized helping them could be a very good thing for the honest silversmiths trying to make a living. He sure didn't appreciate the methods though.

"Tell you what," he replied. "I'll do it on one condition. My wife and all her relatives that are weavers are off your so-called list. I will try to help but only using legitimate means and if things get dangerous you have to cut me loose. Deal?"

"I don't see that as being a problem. We play by the rules and I'll keep you out of the line of fire. This is a smart choice, Charlie. As of today, Bloom's Gallery is starting a line of traditional Navajo jewelry. I will get you introduced to Blue and you can begin your education. No one, and I mean *no one* but Blue and yourself can know you're involved in this case. If you blow your cover you could put yourself and your family in real danger. I'm telling you this for your own good. *Understood?*"

"Yes, I understand," Bloom agreed, not liking it. "This is between me and you and Blue. No others will know."

"Alright, then, let's go catch some bad guys. Welcome to the Bureau. You're in for a fun ride."

Bloom was afraid of just that.

CHAPTER 13

BLUE

Jake Johnson, otherwise known as Blue, should have stood six-foot-three but was bent from a kyphosis of his upper thoracic vertebrae, making his actual height closer to five-foot-eleven. Sitting in any chair produced an automatic slouching position. His oversized jaw jutted out reflexively to help support his large head. Remarkably he still looked physically fit, his legs bulging out of his Levi jeans. Not a man who would tire easily.

At sixtysomething, Blue was proud of his southern roots and maintained his heritage with a Robert E. Lee-style, well-manicured grey beard, stained yellow around his mouth from years of chewing tobacco. He wore a large silver ring adorned with a translucent blue turquoise stone, its color a dead match for his vibrant blue eyes which were the source of his moniker. Those eyes still sparkled of life despite his weathered appearance.

Blue extended his enormous mitt of a hand upon meeting the six-foot-one Bloom that afternoon at Blue's small warehouse office off Cerrillos Road. Bloom, having just turned 50 and still possessing a full head of thick, straight brown hair as well as an upright posture, looked considerably younger than the battered stone man.

"Bloom, hear I need to babysit you for a couple of weeks. Hope you're a fast learner, 'cause there's a shitload to know." As Blue shook Bloom's hand aggressively, he cocked his head, obviously sizing him up.

"Yes," Charles agreed. "Sounds like we're both enlisted whether we like it or not. I'll do my best to learn the jewelry trade."

Blue seemed unsure how much Charles knew of his predicament with the IRS, but he probably assumed he must know the law was not his friend. Charles figured his remark would loosen up Blue and make it clear he was not doing his part willingly, either. Maybe he also was fighting tax problems, not uncommon in the art business. He would keep it vague for now.

"We'll need some luck," Blue acknowledged. "Hope you're smart. These fucking fakers are good and they're doing some shit I ain't seen before and I've seen it all. Most of these silversmiths are going to know me and wonder what I'm doing with a tenderfoot like you. I figure we play it as we're maybe kin and since you recently married a Navajo squaw I needed to teach you the ropes. You got money so we're going to start a business together. You're going to do the buying."

Bloom was shocked at Blue's use of the word *squaw*, but figured he was some old-school dimwit that didn't know any better so he overlooked the offensive remark, at least for now. "So what exactly is it that I need to know, Mr. Johnson?"

"Oh shit, boy, you need to know 30 years of how to handle the back end of a forge. You got to understand what's been made for the last 50 years in the jewelry world, plus what's coming out on the market today. That's all, and we only got a few days to get you up to speed. By the way, don't ever call me Mr. Johnson again. Everyone calls me Blue, like my eyes."

Charles felt his stomach turn. As an art dealer, he understood the difficulty in trying to master the intricacies of any field and the jewelry business seemed harder than most.

After four exhausting hours with Blue, they both had had enough and would start up again bright and early tomorrow. Bloom called Rachael and told her he would be a couple of days later coming home. He gave no explanation other than his gallery needed more clean up, but he suspected she could tell from his voice that something wasn't quite right and also knew he wasn't ready to share. Bloom hoped Blue would never have the pleasure of meeting his wife. *Squaw* was not a word she could brook with. If Blue uttered it in her presence, no telling how she'd set him straight.

Bloom understood all too well that in a few days he was going to be going undercover and was afraid Simplton wasn't giving him the whole picture as to what he might run up against. He decided to try and track down Lieutenant Poh. The way Bloom saw it, that cop had caused the cascade of events by identifying the jewelry as spurious. Maybe Poh could shed some additional light on what Bloom needed to know in his new role as informer.

Since it was late afternoon, Bloom decided he would drop by the station in person. The officer at the front desk told him Poh had gone home for a long weekend. Bloom, the consummate salesman, was able to talk a cell phone number out of a sergeant who overheard the conversation. Santa Fe was a small town and most everyone had heard of Bloom's Art Gallery. Bloom dialed Poh's number from his car.

Poh answered his cell right away. After a brief introduction, Bloom felt comfortable enough to launch into his tale of his own FBI involvement. He knew he wasn't supposed to share this information, but Poh was, so to speak, in the enforcement family and already involved, right? Poh's demeanor was nicer than Bloom anticipated, not all business. The cop unexpectedly invited Bloom out to his house for a firsthand look at why he had been able to spot the fakes.

The sun was setting over Black Mesa as Bloom drove down the bumpy, single-lane dirt road heading onto the fringes of San Ildefonso Pueblo, north of Santa Fe. Bloom had seen the sacred mesa many times as he played his occasional golf match at his favorite course, Black Mesa, located on nearby Santa Clara Pueblo. The back nine abutted the ancestral borders of S.I., as the locals called San Ildefonso. He had often gazed over at the tiny pueblo at the base of the iconic tabletop hill as he waited to hit his approach shot on hole 10. Bloom knew little about the pueblo except that the famous potter Maria Martinez had been from there and with her husband Julian had made their highly collectable black-on-black ceramics. Bloom had recently considered carrying her undecorated 1960s gunmetal finished pots, as they were rather contemporary in appearance and would complement his gallery's art. Unfortunately the high quality of her pots also made them expensive and he wasn't sure he could buy enough work to make an impact.

As dusk turned to evening, he wished he were searching for Maria's relatives on a buying mission now and not to meet a cop to discuss his role as an informant for the FBI.

Poh's directions were similar to those he often received on the Navajo Rez. "Turn at the blue mailbox, go up past two dirt roads, and look for the second sign that says 'black pottery for sale.' Make sure it's the second sign, then take a right, heading south till you see my truck. It has a police light on top. You can't miss it."

That final phrase insisting "you can't miss it" was usually the harbinger that he would be guaranteed to go awry. But three years living on the rez had given Bloom the capability to visualize these enigmatic maps and find his way to locales where Google maps would never work.

A tall, handsome man with cropped black hair graying at the temples, attired in jeans and a sweatshirt, matching Poh's police department photograph was waiting for him near the aforementioned truck.

Hesitating for a moment, not knowing whether it was considered impolite not to wait a minute before getting out of his vehicle like it was back home, Bloom decided to proceed with his task since it was getting darker by the moment. He got out of his pickup and launched in, "Thanks for inviting me out on such short notice, Lieutenant Poh. I really appreciate it."

"No problem, and please call me Billy. I'm off duty as you can probably tell by my civilian clothes. Got a few rare days to myself. I've been to your gallery. I visited one Indian Market weekend a long time ago to see Willard Yellowhorse's paintings. He was an amazing artist. Of course I could only dream about owning a piece. I was just a kid in school. My mom dragged me in. She said I needed to see this guy's work and like always, Mom was right. I did get a poster. I'll show it to you when we go into my studio."

Bloom nodded his head. "It's a small world, isn't it? My mom told me I would go into the arts when I was just a kid and she was right, too. Seems like a lifetime ago, doesn't it? Willard was certainly special. You might find this of interest: I ended up marrying his sister Rachael and she's as talented a weaver as her brother was a painter."

"Good for you, a good Indian woman will do wonders as far as keeping your attitude in check."

Both men smiled, knowing exactly what was meant.

Bloom continued, "In fact, Billy, it's an attitude adjustment that I'm trying to avoid. I told you over the phone what the FBI is asking me to do. What I didn't share was the way they want me to do it. A list of sorts is being compiled to round up Diné that might be considered suspects and I was told politely to help or I would end up on this so-called list, and I'm not allowed to tell my wife about any of this, so I'm hoping you might help me understand more about what I'm getting myself into."

"Yeah, sorry to hear that, but these shenanigans happen all too frequently. I wish I could say it's limited to the FBI, but it's not. So what do you want to know exactly?"

Bloom got right to the point. "Well, first of all, what's your take on this fake jewelry, and secondly, why is this stuff being circulated?"

Poh held up a finger. "Come into my shop I'll show you how I knew that work was fake."

Bloom followed Poh into a small but meticulously clean studio. Every tool had its own place and all were lined up in neat lines, graduated by size. The worn, white linoleum was spotless. As promised, a poster of a Willard Yellowhorse *chindi* painting hung over Poh's massive drill. It was clear Billy Poh was a neat freak and a fan of Bloom's former star artist. The two talked of Yellowhorse and how the painting was chosen for the poster, then Billy took time to show Bloom the tools he used and the methods he employed to make his jewelry, methods he assured were similar to how the Diné smiths also worked.

"I see," Bloom commented. "So, the particular way of stamping and the way the bracelet fits together were tip-offs for you?"

"Yes. If you handle enough pieces, or in my case make enough, the silver speaks to you. With regards to the 'why' I can't say. From what you told me there is no way it makes economic sense. The fact the FBI has taken such a prominent role in delving into this situation is also out of the ordinary. We have been trying for years to stop those cheap fakes from cropping up around the Plaza and have asked repeatedly for a show of force, and nada. Then this happens and out of nowhere we've got an upper-level FBI agent stationed here for the foreseeable future. In my experience, that means something else is going down that they aren't telling us. I would keep my guard up if I were you and hope your wife doesn't find out what's going down. The less she knows, probably the better, at least for now. It's bad enough that they've got you playing double agent, you don't want to drag your wife into a bad situation."

Bloom nodded. "Thanks, I owe you one. Why don't you show me some more of your jewelry. You never know, I might need a good silversmith at the gallery sometime."

Poh spent an additional half-hour showing Bloom his current inventory.

Bloom bumped his way out of the pueblo in complete darkness, letting his headlights guide him. In some ways, he felt more confused than when he arrived. His inner angst had ratcheted up a notch and there was no way to diffuse it. Just as he had suspected, Shirley Simplton was not telling him everything and it wasn't clear if she would anytime soon.

CHAPTER 14

ON A NEED-TO-KNOW BASIS

Simplton wasn't from Santa Fe. She worked with the FBI's art fraud department in Washington, D.C. Her accent and demeanor betrayed her East Coast roots. The "art squad," as they called themselves, was a poorly funded section of the force. Considering the billion-dollar implications that were involved with art theft and fraud, the department was surprisingly minuscule, with only 13 agents to cover all the world's art crimes. Simplton's area of expertise was undercover work, predicated on her double major in art history and criminal justice.

Her usual assignment was as the pretty mistress with the supposedly mega-wealthy older billionaire looking to add to his private collection. She didn't mind being treated as the toy as long as everyone involved got busted and she got to put the handcuffs on first. It gave her a rush she liked to reproduce in the bedroom.

Unfortunately, her last few ops hadn't gone as planned. Two years ago, Simplton was working the biggest case of her career. The Russian Bratva, also known as the Solntsevskaya Brotherhood organized crime gang, was trying to secure three early impressionist paintings worth $100 million euros in lieu of an outstanding drug debt. Stolen art is a great commodity for collateral for drugs or money. It has value, but only at a very reduced level. In Simplton's case, a drug dealer wanted to pay off his loan with the paintings, which they recently stole from a Dutch museum. Simplton and her partner had intercepted the Bratva henchmen going to negotiate the trade. They assumed their respective roles and went in for the arrest.

However, the art thieves who had meticulously planned the museum robbery were more sophisticated than anticipated and recognized the switch and instead of the bad guys being caught, her partner was executed, shot in the head in front of her. These men didn't play nice. After three days of hell, Simplton was dumped naked in a back ally in Moscow with the warning, "Don't fuck with us, next time we kill both," scratched in her back, deep enough to read.

After spending three months recovering, Simplton had resumed her duties working at a desk for a year. She had gotten a commendation for bravery but she believed to climb further up the ranks, she had to prove herself worthy. When the Bureau got the call from Lieutenant Poh, Simplton recognized this might be her opportunity.

Dealing with fake jewelry was beneath her, usually junior agent domain, but this case was different. What she hadn't shared with Bloom or Blue was that her contacts overseas had provided evidence of who was involved in the jewelry production and if they were correct, it was a big fish, the kind that could make a career, *her career*. A large number of sophisticated jewelers had been recruited all at one time in the Baltics. This group of highly skilled men had left their families to work on a secret project and been sequestered by an international conglomerate. The men were sending sizable checks to their families.

The apparent funding had been traced to a South African source based in Johannesburg. This bank handled multinational companies with huge payrolls. It was odd that such a large institution would be going through back channels to provide funds to a rinky-dink operation seeded in the Baltic.

The possible connection was stumbled upon when a family member complained she couldn't get in touch with her father and then the story of the clandestine jewelry came out.

Simplton's source was inside the police department in Belgrade. He told her that it seemed strange how the police treated the incident seriously when the family member first filed a complaint, but then it seemed to be hushed up. All this was a long shot, but the timing of jewelry coming from an unknown source of a high quality was too much to be a coincidence, something Simplton didn't believe in.

Simplton was working the Belgrade connection and hadn't traced down the exact money source, but in her experience in South Africa dubious operations equated to trouble. Bloom and Blue might very well be walking into more than they could imagine, but for now she couldn't risk divulging too much information. She needed them on board. Bloom was cautious by nature. If it looked to be a multinational syndicate, he would bolt, list or no list. For now, giving him information would be only on a need-to-know basis until she understood who and what she was dealing with.

More than anything, Simplton was looking to move up the ranks and this case could be her first-class ticket to department head. She wouldn't let Bloom screw it up by bailing too early in the game. Besides, he was cute.

CHAPTER 15

HE'S NOT TELLING ME EVERYTHING

It was coming up on two weeks since Rachael had seen Bloom, the longest they had been separated in their three-year relationship, all because of a broken water pipe, or so he said. Their nightly talks helped dull the loneliness of missing a soul mate's touch, but did nothing to eliminate the mind-numbing pain which reared its ugly head at 1am.

This was when Sam's unhappy cries invariably erupted. Her high-pitched colicky predilections were the alarm clock no mother likes to hear. The nightly routine seemed to have intensified since Bloom left, though in reality it was probably the same. Only Rachael's warm shoulder would ease the newborn's discomfort. The rocking back and forth gave Sam and Rachael both time to reflect: Sam on why it hurt to drink milk and Rachael on not having a husband's companionship.

Willy's turn at disruption was delivered in the form of a hunger call right at 6am. Like his younger sister and father, Willy was prompt. Morning cereal and milk was needed. Rachael's staccato sleep patterns were rendered on her face in the form of large, dark circles underneath her deep brown eyes. She could live with not looking her best, after all who was there to see? But the sleep deprivation had started to affect her weaving skills, something which she couldn't tolerate in herself.

Perfection in her work was a given. It was who she was. Twice in the last week she had made mistakes in her weft color selection. The amateurish errors, as she considered them, had not been noticed until an hour of additional work had been rendered. It had cost her two hours of work each time to painstakingly remove the errant wefts and replace them with correct color combinations. Most would have not noticed the error in color, but Rachael would, which would have bothered her immensely. Her weavings, like her children, needed to be given the best possible effort and for Rachael to be satisfied as an artist meant redoing the color runs.

It seemed of late as if all elements of life were challenging her good nature. The current weather pattern that had settled into the Chuska Valley was one of frigid air, no global warming detected on Navajo lands. The daily highs had presently been near 30 degrees with lows dipping to near-zero.

With wind chills often well below zero, it made for a dangerous environment for her family flock of sheep. Extra time was needed for throwing additional hay and making sure the water tank's ice was broken. Shelter needed to be checked twice a day. She hadn't replaced her last sheep dog in over a year. Bloom had been happy to pick up the slack. He enjoyed the sheep and it gave him a sense of pride in his wife's rugs to tend to the sheep that originated the whole process. But without Bloom, she needed a couple of dogs. In fact, she needed a couple of dogs just in case. Husbands weren't as reliable as good rez dogs. When had she forgotten that?

Rachael's sheep were her family as much as Willy and Sam, so their welfare was of great import. Without their prized wool, her rugs wouldn't have the same luster and color. The sheep contributed her artist's palette. They were irreplaceable. The loss of a single sheep could be problematic down the road. Her loomed rug that she had been referring to lately as "Thelma" was calling for her attention. She had named it in honor of a cantankerous grandmother that liked to hang out at the post and always wanted something from somebody. Like a writer who feels the need to write, Rachael felt cheated if she didn't get to her loom at least a few hours each day. It was still six months till Indian Market, but the money that would be coming from Thelma was pre-spent as Rachael's truck was on its last legs.

Bloom and Rachael had already allocated the August money. Being alone now, she was starting to feel the pressures of family and money even more heavily. Family she could deal with, but money was usually a secondary thought. Bloom had gone up to fix the broken pipe himself to save money but Rachael couldn't help but feel that there was more to it.

Rachael knew she had been pushing pretty hard for a third child. She had always hoped for a triad of small children and her proverbial clock was ticking now that she was in her mid-thirties. Bloom was resistant and it seemed in her mind that the whole broken pipe scenario had been a welcome means to an end for him. He could escape the barrage of baby talk intermixed with real baby cries as well as the burden of discussing the never-ending no child left behind scenario Rachael couldn't help but preach. In her heart, Rachael knew she would be happy with two children and if it became too much of an issue she would drop it, but for now it was still her number one-dinner topic.

Preston, now 18, was on Rachael's mind nearly as much as Bloom. She had raised her late brother's son as her own, and the last two years had been hard on both of them. He had broken up with his girlfriend and subsequently changed college from one in Arizona to another in New Mexico. She texted him often and was looking forward to seeing him home over the upcoming President's Day weekend. His presence would also bring a break from sheep duty for Rachael and by that time Bloom would be home to help with the kids, too. This Friday, the start of President's Day weekend, was Valentine's Day, and there would be no way Bloom would miss Valentine's Day.

It wasn't until Bloom's phone call today announcing more delays that Rachael began to worry that her home life might be more unsettled than she had imagined. She hoped it was her sleep-deprived mind gone wild, but like her children, Bloom was a creature of habit and the timing of the phone call was off.

Bloom called at five o'clock, not seven, their usual time, and he seemed preoccupied. He only talked for a few minutes then said he needed to go, that he had a meeting. None of the usual small talk and he didn't even ask about the kids.

An evening meeting seemed unlikely in the dead of winter. It was dark by five and the roads in Santa Fe were as icy as on the rez. Yet Rachael had not pried any further. Three years living with the same man and you get the sense when something isn't quite right, and this was what Rachael was feeling. Bloom had ended the conversation by saying he might be a couple more days late, hopefully no longer. To her knowledge, the plumbing issue had been fixed and when pressed as to why he would not be coming back home tomorrow as promised, he was evasive. No concrete explanation, just "stuff came up" and he was sorry but would finish as fast as possible and give her a call tomorrow.

Rachael was a woman who followed her gut and her gut was saying, "Bloom is bending the truth." She trusted him completely as far as his commitment to her. It was obvious that he was very much in love. Yet still, there was something amiss.

That night at her 1am think session with the baby, Rachael for the first time entertained the thought that maybe Bloom was having problems with living on the rez, perhaps a cultural clash that he had run into and didn't know how to discuss with her? Why else was he postponing coming home? Living on the rez for a *bilagaana* could be a hard adjustment, a different way of life and people.

By the end of the rock-a-bye session with Sammy, she decided that Bloom simply needed more "me" time to himself, something she could live with. After all, he had been a bachelor for most of his adult life and two small children could make a tiny home even smaller.

Santa Fe had art, food, and social connections. Every time they had gone out on the town, Bloom would meet someone he knew. He had deep connections to Santa Fe.

The reservation was more spread out and less populated, and the only communal meeting center was the Toadlena Trading Post, not exactly Santa Fe's Plaza or Tomasita's for a margarita and chile rellenos. Rachael had a small but close group of relatives and friends, all people she was deeply connected to, but Bloom didn't really know anyone here other than a few of her family members and Sal Lito, the Toadlena trader, and Carson Riddly, their family doctor and friend in Kayenta. All but Sal and Carson were Diné. Rachael reasoned that Bloom was still trying to understand what being Diné meant. She knew Willy's laughing ceremony had inspired Bloom's overall concept of family and *hozho*. Seeing so many people wishing him and his family good luck in their son's life had been profoundly stirring for Bloom. It had been a watershed moment for them both.

Well, he probably just needed a temporary break. Being back in his own gallery and renewing his art-world ties must be what Bloom craved. It could be as simple as wanting to hear English instead of a constant chatter in Diné. To take this extra time away from him or force him home sooner than he wanted might drive a divide between them. He must want something she couldn't offer. She would be patient.

However, if Bloom missed Valentine's Day, then she would have to come to grips with the fact that something more sinister might be at play. Charles Bloom was a romantic and she knew it. He would come home in time for his Valentine's treat. He had never missed bringing her a card, flowers, or candy, and sometimes all three.

After putting Sammy back to bed, she climbed under the covers she usually shared with Bloom and conjured up his presence in her mind, replaying their five o'clock conversation and what it all meant. If she still had doubts in the morning, then she would do some investigating. For now, though, she'd let Bloom be Bloom, a *bilagaana* married to a strong-minded Diné woman.

CHAPTER 16

FEBRUARY 10, PACK BACK JACK

February in Tucson is a dichotomy of weather; it can be beautiful or rainy. Today it chose both, with a California front blowing though the Sonoran Desert right on schedule.

"Goddamn rain. Always happens during the Gem and Mineral Show. Can't wait a few fucking weeks," the big-bellied man said to no one in particular. "Man's got to make a livin' and it's damn hard when mother nature's got it in for you along with all the freaking fakers from Thailand."

Pack Back Jack was a fixture from the sixties with his unkempt beard juxtaposed against a silver mane neatly tied back in a bun, secured with a chunk of Bisbee turquoise, the stone coming from his first big score. Like all stone men, he answered by a moniker. His was Pack Back Jack. It had been shortened to just "Pack" by those in the know. He had gone by Pack or Jack for so long, no one knew his birth name, which was fine by him.

Pack always wore the same heavy leather backpack in the same exact position, slung over his left side, for 40 years. The process of carrying the heavy pack had led his shoulder and neck muscles on that side to become noticeably larger. The pack was dirty grey in color, having never being washed, other than by the occasional spilled beer or sudden downpour. Its original tan shade was long obliterated. When the backpack's flaps were inverted, shades of various blue and green stones appeared on cue. The colorful rocks were organized by turquoise mines. They represented the best stones he had amassed over a lifetime. He was the quintessential stone man. Pack lived to find better examples of turquoise nuggets to add to his mobile museum.

The stones acted as his grading standard for turquoise. Flip over one of the many flaps and there was an example of a high-grade natural turquoise cabochon. He had all the rare examples: Bisbee, Lander, Turquoise Mountain, #8. There were hundreds of stones and a few larger trade pieces. It was his legacy and workbench combined, thus the pack never left his side, not even to sleep. Pack had taken to the idea of keeping his wealth on him from trading with Navajos, who he observed often kept their wealth close at hand or arm, as the case may be.

The Tucson Gem and Mineral Show is loaded with turquoise, the largest single venue in the world. The official show takes place on the second full weekend of February at the Tucson Convention Center, but for the two weeks leading up to it, all the top turquoise dealers show up en masse like the swallows of Capistrano. Stone men from every part of the globe sell and trade from their hotel rooms, offering stones they've gathered over the last year. A few of the wealthiest just shop for themselves or clients.

Jack was on the lower end of the evolutionary spectrum, not a Lander turquoise guy, but more your run-of-the-mill Nevada stone trader. He resented those who had made the big score. He neither had the discipline nor the knowledge, but he still felt slighted. His education had been at the working end of a shovel in wildcat mines throughout the Southwest. Once he had a nice turquoise claim in Madrid, New Mexico, just outside Santa Fe, then it collapsed after a huge monsoon storm. It was the closest he had gotten to climbing to the next level. The gods were against him then, as they were today.

Pack's face was not unlike the stones he collected, with rough, deep grooves from unabated sun exposure, never having bothered with wide-brim hats or sunscreen, which he considered a waste of time not to mention money. Other bad habits would kill him long before the sun. His thick fingers and unkempt beard had permanent yellow stains from years of Camel cigarette abuse, a trait common among stone men.

While most saw him as a hard man, Pack never missed the opportunity to share his walking museum with kids, including giving them a free little turquoise nugget to pique their interest in something he loved so much. He wanted to share his passion, hoping he was not the last of a dying breed of rock hounds. Looking at those who were still in the business, it appeared the days of his ilk were numbered.

Since money was not to be made sitting in his cramped hotel room waiting for the weather to turn, Pack locked the sliding-glass window, jammed a rod in the bottom groove for extra security, then put out his hand-lettered sign that said "Back Soon" and grabbed a handful of his lower-end turquoise strands and his recycled golf bucket of raw nuggets and hit the pavement. He began wandering up the cheap hotel strip west of interstate I-10 looking for any kind of action. The rain would have been welcome any other time to this man of the desert, but today it just solidified his low place in the food chain where every sale counted.

There were a dozen marginal hotels lining I-10. For two weeks in February, rock hounds become the lifeblood of Tucson's shadier lodging establishments, displacing meth heads and prostitutes with higher-paying renters. Thousands of vendors from around the world congregate, bringing with them all types of gems, minerals, and fossils to vie for the $100 million of buyer money which streams into the Tucson economy. The worn-down hotels take on the atmosphere of bazaars in Africa.

"Got any good nuggets? Anything new? Ready to trade some nice jaculas," Pack yelled at another stone man, a fellow known as Nevada, as the rain pelted his face, causing his words to spew moisture. Pack's neck was draped with multiple Sleeping Beauty turquoise necklaces. The Diné call them jaculas and they are highly cherished.

"Nah, Pack, ain't seen nothin' to speak of. Got nothin' I can trade for either, unless you need an umbrella?" Nevada laughed at Pack's wet-dog appearance and desperate attempt to make something happen. "Hey, maybe this is worth something to you. The President ain't showed up yet. He's five days late. Not like him. Here's the interesting part. I heard a rumor he's hunting a claim, maybe the best ever seen." The scruffy man tried to catch his breath in the damp air.

"You're messing with me. You're just saying that to get my juices going 'cause we're both pissed off about this rain," Pack said, huddling with his colleague.

Both of them lit up, sharing their mutual Camel cigarette addiction.

"Nah, wouldn't do that to you, Pack. I knows you want to add to your little traveling museum so I figured I'd give you the heads up. Maybe if it turns out to be true you can toss me a little nugget for my good info or one of those nice jaculas you got there."

"Hell, if it's true and it's what you say it is and if I score, I'll toss you something better than one of these cheap tourist necklaces. I'll give you a cherry Cerrillos cab I've been saving. Found it myself when I still had my Madrid mine." Pack opened his museum flap like a peep show and pointed to a pinpoint greenish polished stone.

"Deal!"

After the last of the cigarettes' nicotine cloud dissipated into the creosote-filled air, Pack sauntered down the wet road avoiding the larger puddles, his spirits slightly lifted. *The best ever seen*, was it? Those words played in his head. His mind was made up. Directly after the show he would be on the President's trail.

As it would turn out, he wouldn't be the only one.

CHAPTER 17

LOAD OUT

There was only one good retail sale for Pack at the gem show that year, to a man from the exclusive Loew's Ventana Canyon Resort area. Pack had delivered it himself, carting the two large barrels of raw turquoise up a winding concrete road behind the members' lodge. Perched precariously in the Santa Catalina Mountains was an ultramodern home of glass and steal. Pack assumed the guy was an amateur rock hound to purchase so much rock, but once there he realized the fellow must be some crazy art collector. The guy had Pack dump the stones out at various locations around the property where they tumbled halfway down the slopes, only stopping when hitting a cactus or scraggly mesquite tree. "Landscape art," the guy called it. Pack thought it was bullshit but he could care less since the client paid in cash and didn't ask for a discount. It would be enough money to get Pack through March if he was careful.

In the show's final hours, a very peculiar man came through looking for the President. His accent said foreigner and his physique said athlete. The man sought out Pack. Pack said he was planning to touch base with the President directly after the show and then the man with the funny- sounding accent did the oddest thing. He handed

Pack a crisp $100 bill, along with a hard-stock business card imprinted "CXI, Max Solenhosen, 505.820.7451." Pack figured it must be a Santa Fe or Albuquerque number.

"Call me when you run into your Mr. President. I will get you another $100 for your trouble, Mr. Pack. Just call me as soon as you know his whereabouts. We can keep this between you and me." The fellow smirked at Pack as if saying it was their little secret.

Pack was no fool. This fellow wanted something big time and only the President had it. Pack, trying to make his own big sale, offered the man every possible stone, showing him his entire museum collection.

"Thank you, Mr. Pack, but I need to speak with Mr. President, soon I hope. If you do find him, I will spend some monies on your finer turquoise. Maybe I will buy your whole museum, come up with a price for its entire contents. But first, find Mr. President. Call me. We all will win." He lightly punched Pack in a friendly fashion on his non-enlarged arm. The man's strength was palpable. Then he nodded, as if to seal the deal. Pack disliked him on the spot, as he despised all men of wealth that possess a self-assured ease, which Max Solenhosen obviously had. Yet the thought of selling his museum made finding the President that much more important.

Whatever the President had, it must be monumental. No one hands out $100 dollar bills unless they are crazy, very rich, or working something big. Little did the man with the funny accent know that Pack had his own plans for the President and he couldn't or wouldn't call him until he had what he wanted. Pack didn't own a phone, never had, never would, but he had something the rich guy didn't, the intimate knowledge of the habits of one "Stonicus manicus."

This morning, Pack reluctantly turned to the task at hand: load out. All dealers, no matter what material they handle, hate load out. It's the time when all the things that didn't sell must be packed up and taken back home. Whether it's the highest-end items or just lowly tubs of turquoise rocks, it can be depressing, not to mention hard work. The end of the show is a time of reflection. For Pack this year, the realization was that his hope to score the big deal had evaporated once more and all that was left for his last day in Tucson was the tending of his failing back. A strong back that in his younger years could easily handle a 100-pound load of rocks was now tested daily by his 35-pound backpack. At 65, Pack was nearing the end of his traveling-and-carrying lifestyle.

Finding the President was paramount. If Pack could complete his mobile museum with one final great stone, maybe he could sell the whole collection and have something for his retirement. There would never be any Social Security for the man who only dealt in cash, having never had a real job to speak of. He was coming to the conclusion that he would definitely need to sell his museum if he planned to survive past 70.

In the rock trade, turquoise is often sold by the pound, not the nugget, thus wholesaling large quantities of rocks of equivalent grade which can be made into finer-grade cabochons. The sort of lower-grade material that Pack dealt in was turquoise that would probably end up having plastic filler added to make stabilized tourist jewelry, the kind that is notoriously sold around the fringes and sometimes not-so-fringes of Santa Fe's Plaza, as much plastic as turquoise. Pack possessed 10 barrels of raw blue laced rock, each weighing 400 pounds. To load these out, there was only one way, brute force. The three large cases used to show off some of the better-grade material were heavy but not like the raw ore, plus of course there was his omnipresent Pack museum, all of which had to be fitted into his aging Ford pickup and hauled back to his Gallup trailer home and unloaded. The trailer, which had seen better days and was located in a less-than-desirable part of town, would be a six-hour drive from Tucson.

It was no coincidence that Gallup was "stone man central," the place that most of the self-sustaining individuals who craved the blue demon called home. Like New York's diamond traders, they went where their livelihood was. The turquoise dealers set roots in the heart of Indian jewelry country, and Gallup it was. Not even big shots like the President could resist Gallup's lapidary charms. Numerous Navajo silversmiths in close proximity to great rocks with the skills to make quality jewelry and an ample supply of stonecutters made it their Mecca. Plus, Gallup was situated smack in between the major Southwest hubs of Santa Fe, Phoenix, Flagstaff, and Tucson, so it only required a day's drive to most of the important retail outlets.

For now, the Tucson Quality Inn, which was anything but quality, had to be vacated by 1pm. That meant the whole exhibit had to be loaded to hit the road in four hours. It was a task no dealer likes, especially after a less than stellar two weeks of selling.

The President's no show was a first as far as Pack could remember, which confirmed that he must be on to something big, or possibly dead. The President's usual modus operandi was to make an early appearance at the gem show, orchestrate some significant purchases, entertain his big clients, then retreat to Gallup to reload and start cutting the stones he had procured. The stone men that set up at Gem and Mineral would cull their best stones all year and wait for the gem show, knowing the frenzy of the event would help sell more stones at higher prices.

They all counted on seeing the President. He was part of the magic sauce. He dropped money throughout the show, paid fairly, and kept prices strong, but not this year. One other stone man had echoed Nevada's tip but Pack wasn't sure this wasn't just recycled info making the rounds. Nevada, who wanted to secure his position in order to obtain his Cerrillos kicker, reported back to Pack that he heard from a reliable source that the President had already had had stones cut and had sold a killer dark blue cab to an important client. All Pack knew was that for the President not to be scouring the gem show, a place you could always score at least one great find, meant something suspicious was afoot. Pack planned on investigating tomorrow once he got back to Gallup. His main concern, like usual, was to find the President before he sold all his best stones, thus potentially depriving Pack's traveling museum of a rare find. The small thread of happiness Pack had experienced just a few days earlier was turning to doubt now.

Maybe I have lost my opportunity, all the great shit already spoken for. Won't be able to sell my museum if I don't have the very best.

Brooding wouldn't help anything. "*Andale! Andale!* Move your butts. I got to get on the road. If you want my hard-earned dollars instead of pesos, you best get going," Pack yelled at the Mexican day laborers he had secured from the side of the I-10. Pack generally was not racially belligerent, having spent so much time in New Mexico, but it was load out and not a happy one. In fact, it was the worst he could remember, what with his anger at the President for not showing, a less than stellar show, and his back feeling much older than 65. Sad to realize, Pack didn't have many load outs left in him.

After four hours of hard work by all, his truck and trailer were buttoned down. He handed the two men each a $50 bill and tossed each man a bottle of cold Corona and some venison jerky and thanked them for their efforts. No apologies were spoken but it was obvious Pack was trying to make amends for being such a *pendejo*.

Yes, his first order of business would be finding the President: start in Gallup, if no luck there then hit Toadlena, Shiprock, Farmington, and if need be all the posts in Arizona and New Mexico until a scent of his trail turned up. Great stones were Pack's food. He would find the breadcrumbs. He always did.

CHAPTER 18

THE BIRD

The lessons on turquoise were a mind blower for Bloom, who had no idea that there were so many varieties of turquoise mines and that the subtle differences between them could be so significant. Bloom's innate sense of color, so critical in modern art, helped him. Blue doled out a rare compliment on day two when Bloom separated the Turquoise Mountain stones from the Morenci, discerning the differences quickly. In an odd way, Bloom enjoyed mastering these intricacies even if they had to come in the form of a command interaction with the politically incorrect Blue.

Bloom was starting to understand the lingo of the turquoise trade: buzz names like Bisbee Blue, #8, and Lander. The mines producing the best stones were the easiest to recognize.

Today they also covered construction techniques of jewelry and bezels, the silver enclosures that hold the stones. Bloom quickly was able to distinguish good workmanship from poor, his art training once again providing similarities when it came to determining quality. It seemed that he might be able to pull off his charade of wanting to start carrying jewelry in his gallery. Bloom knew the hardest part of being a successful art dealer was not the art but what to pay for inventory. Adapting this concept to jewelry was an important part of his undercover assignment. He had to be able to distinguish a fake and price would be one of the considerations.

The itinerary called for Bloom to return to Toadlena tomorrow. He would let Rachael know of his new business model to carry jewelry and see if Preston—Rachael's nephew who she had raised as a son—would be willing to help out over President's Day weekend by earning some serious extra money. He knew Rachael would be skeptical. Where was the money coming from? Wasn't it a risky departure from his core business? Bloom was not a man to lie by nature. His mother had drummed it into his head to tell the truth, which made his ruse that much more difficult to pull off. He told himself, "I'm doing this for my family. I will come clean when we catch the bad guys." Bloom knew all too well about bad guys and that sometimes they could play rough, very rough, if you got in their way. He hoped bringing in Preston didn't turn out to be a major mistake. If the teenager got hurt in any way, Rachael would never forgive him. It could even end their marriage.

"OK, let's go through it one more time," Blue suggested, as if Bloom were still in junior high.

"I've got it," Bloom assured. "The bigger the stone, the more matrix, the more value. Breaks and chips hurt. Look for the detail in the craftsmanship."

"What else?"

"Check for silver or gold content. It should be stamped for purity on the piece. Never accept the first offer, as jewelers are expecting you to negotiate."

"Fine, you got the highlights. Now let's test you."

Blue pulled at his own ring, freeing it from his oversized finger and handing it gently to Bloom. "What's the stone? And the workmanship?"

"It's deep-blue, flawless, high dome, looks like maybe a Persian stone. Bezel is tight, very fine. The shank is heavy with some fine cracking in the silver, probably ingot silver. This is good work with an excellent cabochon." Bloom looked inside and saw an unusual maker's mark incised in the ring's belly. It was a human hand irreverently flipping the bird.

"I would think that's not an Indian mark. Seems like it would be a poor way to brand oneself. I'm guessing you made it?"

"Shit, that's good Bloom. How'd ya know it was old Blue's work? And yes it is Persian. I cut the cab myself 30 years ago."

"Well, Blue, you wear that ring on your middle finger for starters and I may not know much, but with no stamp work on the outside and such a fine bezel with a big stone, it didn't seem like it was Navajo. Just my instinctive assessment, I guess."

"Exactamundo, my friend. Remember, that's your best sense. If it don't feel Injun-made, it probably ain't. That's OK if it's good stuff, but you're in the Injun business so if you sell it as Native you're looking at trouble from one of those Fed types. You're ready, my boy. Let's go make a bunch of silversmiths happy and get that spinster Simplton off my fucking back."

CHAPTER 19

HEADING WEST

The drive to Gallup was more treacherous than usual for Charles Bloom on February 13th. Blue's car added additional stress to the trip, the old guy creeping along behind Bloom's truck in a beat-up, mint-green Ford Fiesta. It was hard to believe that Blue could get around in that thing on the rez. Bloom had learned the hard way that the rez could be very hard on cars. Trucks were the vehicles of choice, preferably of the four-wheel-drive variety. The crap car might explain Blue's unusual physical prowess. He must have spent a lot of time hoofing it.

Bloom had sold his beloved Mercedes and put the money into a slightly used four-by-four gold Ram truck with black interior. He was glad for the extra traction as he headed out of Grants with the winter weather near white-out conditions. He suspected he would be pulling his new partner out of a ditch in the near future, but somehow Blue was managing to get through, fishtailing wildly up hills and skidding down.

By the time they arrived on the outskirts of Gallup, the snow that was so prevalent in Grants had all but vanished, leaving little accumulation. The change in weather lifted Bloom's sprits a bit. Even if the land could use the moisture, he was glad it was drying out now, a very un-Navajo thought. The two pulled over for a bathroom break as the skies cleared. They discussed the game plan, their backs against the gas station's north-facing wall, Bloom warming his hands and Blue filling his mouth with a chew.

"Blue, can I ask you why you don't have a truck? You spend a lot of time out on the rez, don't you?"

"Yeah, I know it's squirrelly to have such a piece of shit vehicle, but I've been on a bad streak. Lost my truck in an accident, the insurance company screwed me over, so I've been stuck with this lime lifesaver of a car for nearly two years. But my luck is changing, you'll see. By next year this time I'll have a new truck."

Bloom decided not to dwell on the topic of luck with Blue, who didn't seem to have much of it and as far as Bloom could tell was destined to be driving Old Green for the foreseeable future, but he did admire Blue's attitude. The geezer did have the conviction he would prevail, no matter how unlikely that might be.

Blue planned, "So we drive into Gallup and I'll park at the Lotaburger. We'll take your truck the rest of the way. It's too hard to describe how to get to our next stop. Lots of twisting dirt roads and I don't want you getting lost. We're going to see my old buddy Pack. He's a good stone man. Don't plan on getting out of there anytime soon. Knowing Pack, he'll expect us to stay."

Bloom objected, "I do need to go before it gets dark. My wife is expecting me for dinner, so I can't stay too long with Mr. Pack."

"Your call, but remember you got a lot to learn and Pack knows more than me when it comes to good turquoise. And drop the 'Mr.' shit with us stone men. It's just Pack."

"I understand, Pack, not Mr. I'll stay as long as I can but you don't know my wife."

Blue smirked. Bloom figured he understood all wives were demanding, which was why he had never gotten hitched. Same as Bloom, before he met Rachael.

As he drove into Gallup, Bloom knew Rachael would be expecting him to come home directly from Santa Fe, especially after not seeing her for almost two weeks and what with Valentine's Day tomorrow. He missed his kids and wondered if either child would even remember his face. As much as he loved his children, he wasn't sure he was a good father. He had been a bachelor a long time. It still felt odd to be married with children.

Rachael was everything one could hope for in a spouse: the first to defend him, never complained, and great in bed. They had been together for three years. Lately she had been talking about having one more child and Bloom was feeling pressure, similar to when she wanted to get married. Having an additional mouth to feed and house, not to mention raising one more child at his age, was a daunting proposition. Rachael's hogan was woefully inadequate as it was. A third child would force him to either add a room or move sooner than he planned. There were not many big houses on the rez. He had been gently nudging Rachael to consider relocating to Santa Fe. It seemed a good move. He could get some momentum going again in the gallery while the kids were still young, make enough money to be able to afford a bigger place, and then consider one more child. Her sheep were a problem but not an untenable one. Santa Fe had places for grazing just south of town near La Cienega, which was more affordable. The future of their family was a dilemma he wasn't ready to face now. Purchasing jewelry he didn't want seemed the lesser of two evils.

Such were the thoughts circling in Bloom's mind as he pulled into the Gallup Lotaburger just off Highway 491. Blue parked his green jalopy in the lot. Hopping into Bloom's truck, the big man grunted as he made himself comfortable. He took out a cigar to light, then as Bloom looked his way, began chewing on it instead.

"Cut back on my cigar smoking lately," Blue commented. "Kinda hard breathing up there in Santa Fe, the altitude and all." Blue automatically tuned the radio to channel 666 AM to catch up on the latest news. "Hope you don't mind. Been stuck in Santa Fe too long where every fucking channel is NPR or some Mexican mariachi."

"That's fine. It's nice to hear Diné again," Bloom responded to his rude guest and wondered how someone as redneck as Blue could even live in Santa Fe.

Blue gave directions with his hands, pointing each time at the last moment just before it was time to turn. After 20 minutes they arrived at a dilapidated hovel of a trailer. If not for the backstop of a low-slung mesa, the north wind would have surely blown it away. Large pieces of stone in various states of being cut were scattered throughout the property, many showing traces of blue. Bloom figured turquoise was still waiting to be released from their bonds.

Bloom eased his Ram truck up to the front of the trailer.

The old guy with the bun was working out front, his cold breath mixing with the soldering smoke that was emanating from a piece of jewelry he was turning into an "Indian style" bracelet. Pack took pride in his silversmith skills and signed his jewelry "POB." It stood for "Pack on his Back." Pack knew Begay was the most common name on the reservation, like Smith in the *bilagaana* world, so most people would just assume it was Peter or Paul Begay. White men's work didn't get the same respect or money as the Diné pieces, was Pack's thinking. Pack looked uneasily at the unknown vehicle, his right hand tightly gripping a five-pound hammer, which he raised to chest level, revealing an impressive bicep with a tattoo that said "Mother." Not bad for a man of 65.

Blue stuck his arm out of the passenger window, the back of his hand facing Pack, knowing the fellow stone man would recognize a good chunk of turquoise before he would the man.

Pack snorted, "What the fuck, you upgraded your piece of shit car?"

"Wish that was the case, buddy. Still got my baby. She's about down to the last of her miles, I'm afraid. How about I trade you for a couple of good pieces of turquoise in that satchel of yours?" Blue grinned, knowing that Pack would rather die than get rid of museum-grade turquoise.

"How about we don't and you can tell your friends, if you have any, that you did."

Bloom opened his driver's door, unsure how to join the conversation, an unusual occurrence for a man who made his living with his mouth.

"Hey, Pack, nice to meet you. I'm Charles Bloom. Blue tells me I need to talk to you about getting some jewelry that has great turquoise."

Blue gave Bloom a frown, telegraphing Bloom's poor handling of negotiations.

Bloom immediately understood the facial queue, remembering Blue's advice back in Santa Fe: "Let Pack ask the questions. Never be too eager with a stone man like Pack."

Bloom tried to backtrack. "Anyway… I'll let Blue explain, he's the buyer."

Pack narrowed his eyes. "Blue, you buying again? I heard you still owed some guys out of Texas for a bunch of high grade #8? You got cash for this buying? Cash is king. Credit's just for suckers and I ain't no sucker."

Bloom watched Pack eye Blue for any signs of deceit like the flinch of an eye or breaking eye contact.

"I got cash," Blue assured. "Why don't you, me, and Bloom here go inside and have a beer? You still drink, don't you? It's after 1pm and I'm thirsty."

"I drink, so long as you're buying. Got any good rocks to show me?"

Blue pulled out one of the fake bracelets from his shirt pocket and tossed it to Pack. "How about I give you this, will that buy me a beer or two?"

Bloom wondered how Blue had finagled a bracelet from Simplton, and knew she would not be happy at his giving her evidence away for beer.

Pack eyed the piece closely. He smelled it, taking a whiff like it was a fine Bordeaux, and with the tip of his tongue licked the entire turquoise cab. Then he replied, still looking at the bracelet, "No shit, you can give me this for a couple of Old Milwaukee's. It's a nice rock. Don't recognize the mine, but it tastes like it's from around the salt mines just northeast of here. Where'd you get this bad boy? Not Navajo. Are there some new white dudes working my circuit?"

Blue nodded. "That's what I'm here to find out. Me and my partner want to find more of this stuff. It's high quality and we can pawn it off as Navajo to most folks, except an expert like you. I'll cut you in for some of the action if you can find the source. You still packing?"

"Yep, got my museum right here and my enforcer underneath." Pack flipped over a secondary, less noticeable flap of his knapsack, and the butt end of a pistol became visible.

"Let's go drink. We only got four hours before sunset," Pack said, yanking open his trailer door. "Enter the castle." Both men started to laugh.

Bloom's neck hairs stood up as he followed behind the two into the dark, unknown environment that Pack called his castle. Bloom wished he'd headed north first, straight up Route 491 to Toadlena. He missed Rachael and wasn't sure what he was getting himself into. His inner voice was saying, "Go home now—you're a family man not a stone man," but he followed anyway.

CHAPTER 20

HOME FOR PRESIDENT'S DAY WEEKEND

Rachael couldn't wait for Bloom's return. She needed help with the nightly feeding schedule, not to mention Bloom's warm stomach muscles nestled up against her back at bedtime. Her annual Indian Market rug was slowly taking on a personality. She had finished 10 inches of a tapestry weave that would be 60 inches long when complete. At the current pace, there would be plenty of time to finish not only this rug but an additional mat-size weaving before her August show. Completing the small weaving meant baby clothing would be taken care of for the year. Today she couldn't focus on her weaving though, try as she might.

Preston would be home any minute for his four-day break, too. President's Day weekend for some reason was a big deal in Socorro and the Mining Institute gave them Valentine's Day off this year as well as the usual Monday holiday. The whole school was closing down. It had been two months since Rachael had seen Preston Yellowhorse. It didn't seem possible that it would be spring soon. The temperature was still dreadfully cold with occasional snow flurries gracing the two grey hills looming outside her kitchen window. Preston was in his sophomore year at the New Mexico Institute of Mining and Technology, majoring in geology, and she couldn't be prouder.

✲ ✲ ✲ ✲

Preston had already made plans for his entire four-day vacation, plans he was greatly looking forward to. He would be helping Bloom buy jewelry. Bloom had shared his proposal with Preston last night.

Now, Preston came bounding through Rachael's bent-framed front door, tossing it open with abandonment. The frame was permanently damaged, a casualty of Preston's testosterone-filled teenage years.

"Hi, Rach," he yelled, using the name he'd adapted years ago to irritate her but now favored more out of love. "You look like you gained a few pounds. Got that second kid look going. Number three will be coming soon, I bet." He laughed, knowing that this would get her goat better than even the pet name.

"Thanks a lot. Well, you're still as handsome and strong as ever. Come give your Aunty Rachael a hug," she requested, emphasizing the *Rachael* to let him know she caught the jab.

"So what's with the corn tassel?" she teased, touching his goatee.

"That's called a beard and girls dig it," retorted Preston, whose broad shoulders had filled out.

"You got a new girl I should know about?"

Preston had broken up with his longtime Athabascan girlfriend after he transferred out of University of Arizona. He knew Rachael was worried he was lonely going to school in Socorro. "Not currently. Otherwise I wouldn't be home over Valentine's Day weekend, would I? I am, however, growing this beard as an investment for later when I finally do have time for girls. The pickings in the female persuasion are weak in the geology department and that's where I spend most of my time these days."

Then, trying to change the subject, he offered, "You'll be proud of me though. I've been working on my jewelry in my spare time and have got quite a few great pieces finished. I hope Bloom might show my work this summer along with your weavings. I've been trying different stones, ones that aren't, shall we say, traditional. You want to see?"

"Of course. You are a Yellowhorse, so I would expect some exciting fresh work."

Preston pulled out of his pocket five bracelets, all unique and each one exquisitely made, somewhat resembling the sculpture Rachael used to create before returning to her family occupation of weaving rugs. Preston's jewelry was in a style that might be described as Rachael Yellowhorse-meets-Alexander Calder.

The years playing with his Craig Lendskip twine sculpture had influenced Preston's work. The Lendskip sculpture belonged to his late father, Willard Yellowhorse, who was friends with Lendskip. Preston had inherited the valuable piece after Willard's death, not realizing its worth. Bloom had discovered the prized sculpture in a soap dish in the family bathroom, where it had been left by Preston, his favorite toy.

After discerning its authenticity, Bloom and Rachael had placed it on loan at the Navajo Museum in Window Rock with the tag "Private Collection." It would stay safely there, insured, until it was deemed the right time to sell it, if ever. Currently it was insured for $500,000. Preston didn't have a clue as to its value. He just thought it was cool art. Rachael and Bloom had no plans on telling him the true value until he reached 30 and could make a mature decision as to what to do with the piece.

"So what do you think, Rach? You haven't said a word. Don't you like them?"

Tears started to roll down her face. She grabbed her nephew and pulled him close. "They're wonderful! You have a gift I never realized you had. I hate to say it, but you may need to reconsider geology. The silver is calling you. I bet Charles would consider showing your work this summer. We could call it The Rachael and Preston Yellowhorse Show."

"Nice, Rach, but P comes before R alphabetically, so maybe The Preston and Rachael Show?"

Rachael smiled and hugged him tighter. "Nice try, but I'm still the headliner Yellowhorse in the family, at least for now."

CHAPTER 21

THE PLAN

Pack and Blue spent the next two hours discussing old times, none of which Bloom had in common with the two stone men. As best he could determine, these two unique individuals had known each other for over 40 years, meeting at Davis-Monthan Air Force Base in Tucson. Both had fallen in love with Native jewelry and when they got out, each started dealing in Indian jewelry just as the boom hit. The late sixties and early seventies were a gold mine for Indian art dealers, selling overpriced squash blooms and Concho belts to the flower power generation. Not unlike the tulip craze in the Netherlands in 1633, it didn't last long. When the fad faded and Indian jewelry took a tumble, the two stone men switched to dealing in turquoise. When Native jewelry finally did come back in the mid-eighties, the two men were more interested in dealing in turquoise than with silversmiths, though Blue continued to do jobber business to Santa Fe shops on the side.

Blue kept the details of their grand plan for getting into the fake Indian jewelry to a minimum. Pack mainly seemed to care about making money and maybe getting some of the knockoff pieces for his own inventory. Pack knew the locals from Gallup to Shiprock, and made a trip to each trading post and pawnshop once a week as he looked for poorly designed jewelry that was being resold that had great stones. The seventies had produced some of the worst constructed jewelry but great turquoise was coming on the market from newly discovered mines, so amazing stones were incorporated to fill the insatiable appetite for anything Indian. Now Pack looked for these pieces. Pop out the stone, reset in a modern Navajo design, or just sell the cab and melt the silver. It was his bread and butter. Blue was providing an incentive to work harder than usual.

Simplton had come up with the idea, provided the funding, and now Bloom and Blue were putting the plan into motion. Blue was to work with the stone men to find leads, beginning with Pack. For any bracelet Pack found that was like the fakes or obviously containing the same stones, Pack would be paid double what it cost him, up to $85 dollars. Blue knew that Pack would claim the going rate for everything he purchased was $50 regardless of what Pack spent. Pack was strictly a cash kind of guy, so no receipts would be forthcoming. If the vendor who was selling the fakes was turned over as a lead to Blue, Blue would give Pack $15 for any additional pieces he bought from him for one year. Pack could do the math and realized it was in his best interest to score only once with each vendor then turn them over. If it worked, it would mean a lot of free money for Pack, who had never made money sleeping before and seemed to like this idea tremendously.

They decided Pack would check all his favorite spots around Gallup and then meet with them at the Toadlena Trading Post to settle up in one week. Their new jewelry alliance deal was toasted over more beers. Bloom, Blue, and Pack were in business.

Then a subject came up that Bloom knew nothing about, but Blue seemed to find particularly interesting.

"So Blue, you seen the President? He never showed at the Gem and Mineral. Ain't like him," Pack commented.

"Can't say that I have. I spend most of my time in Santa Fe these days. He hasn't come by there, to my knowledge. What do you think's happened? He lives down the street. Have you gone to his house?"

"I've driven by but didn't see his truck so I never stopped. I just got back from the Gem and Mineral and I've been unloading those goddamn barrels of rock, and trying to recover from two weeks on my feet. I plan to go over there tomorrow and snoop around town, maybe stop by PC's. By the way, Blue, you seen any new rocks for my museum? Rumor has it there might be a new one on the market? Fresh find? Something special?"

"Where'd you hear that?"

"Nevada said something about Leroy working on something big and blue."

Blue demurred, "No, hadn't heard that, but you'll be the first to know. I recognize an easy mark when I see him." He laughed at the expense of Pack's obvious interest in new additions to his museum's holdings. Blue was no idiot. The fact that a question about a new find was mentioned nearly in the same breath as the President, who was AWOL, meant something. Pack must believe the President found something and now had made himself scarce. The President was a stone man and would want to brag about something like a major find once it was sewn up, so nobody could steal it. Which meant one thing: if he had made a big score it was still in play. Blue would make his own inquires.

So Bloom surmised, but with his 3pm buzz going he didn't much care. He realized he hadn't learned much about turquoise jewelry, which was the plan, but he did learn stone men like to drink, and hard.

CHAPTER 22

SEE YOU IN A WEEK

The two old cronies were into their third six-pack of Old Milwaukee when Bloom broke up the three-man party. He needed to get home. He was in big trouble already. It was dark now, and it would be worse if he didn't get home by dinner. Rachael was expecting him an hour ago.

Bloom figured he might still be over the legal limit to drive. He had stopped drinking around 3, but with four beers under his belt, even with his height and weight, he would probably blow a .1 alcohol level if a cop pulled him over. He would stop at Lotaburger or the Circle K for something to soak up the alcohol.

"Blue, I need to hit the road. How about I give you a ride back to your car? Or, you have an apartment here, right? Can I drop you off there so you don't have to drive? Then you can meet me up at Toadlena tomorrow."

"Hey, Bloom, I ever tell you I like you, man. You're OK for a fucking suit kinda guy," Blue slurred.

"Thanks Blue, appreciate that. So what do you say? Can I give you a ride?"

"Nope, me and Pack, we got some more stories to swap, and I always like to spend time at his turquoise museum. My shithole apartment's going to be cold as ice. I'd rather stay here. Pack, you care if I bunk with you tonight then you run me into town tomorrow to pick up my car?"

"Sure thing, boss, whatever you say. You're the man, paying my bills this month and maybe a few more after that." The two drunk pals started laughing and Bloom knew it was his moment to escape.

"OK, then I'll see you tomorrow at Toadlena? Say 10am?"

"Bloom, I'm in Gallup and back on Injun time," Blue waved him away. "How about in a week? You know enough to go and buy, so go and buy with that nephew of yours. Pack will round up some fakes by then. Remember, they always want to negotiate. Ain't that right, Pack?"

"Yep, you coulda had me at $75 dollar max on the bracelets, but too late now, old Pack's drunk on the deal."

The two men laughed even louder then and didn't notice as Bloom slipped out.

He was finally heading home to Toadlena. He stopped at the Circle K for breath mints and a rancid cup of coffee. Last thing he needed was a DUI on the reservation. He was a *bilagaana* and being drunk would not go over well. He decided to go to Lotaburger for a green chile cheeseburger to fill up his stomach before he headed up 491, even if it meant more time delays. Rachael would be pissed he had eaten, but she would be even madder if he was taken to jail for drinking.

That would test the relationship, even for a tolerant person like Rachael Yellowhorse.

CHAPTER 23

HELPING OUT

Preston had come home on Friday not only for good home-cooked meals and to see Rachael and the kids, but to make extra cash, lots of it. Bloom had promised him two grand for four days' work, to be exact. The promise of $500 a day for a college sophomore was enticing. It was roughly the same amount he earned for a good silver and turquoise bracelet that took him a week of work to make, not including materials. This was a no brainer. Preston was eager to get going, starting today.

"So when does Mr. Moneybags get home? I'm ready to hit the rez and start helping in the jewelry business."

"You mean my husband, Bloom? He's Mr. Moneybags?"

"Yes, Bloom. In my eyes he sure is Mr. Moneybags, unless two grand doesn't mean anything to a great weaver like yourself?"

"What are you talking about? Two grand for what? And whose jewelry business are you referring to?"

"Uh oh. I can see you and your husband aren't having the best communication these days, so maybe I'll just let you guys talk. Right now I would love one of your great biscuits. You still make those, don't you?"

"In the fridge, next to the milk which has been surprisingly easier to keep in stock since your absence."

"Yeah, I love you too, Rach...." The two sat next to each other eating hot biscuits and drinking milk.

Nothing more was said as the afternoon sun ebbed into darkness. They were both waiting for Mr. Moneybags to appear and he was late, with alcohol on his breath. Valentine's eve was not commencing on a propitious note.

CHAPTER 24

LET ME EXPLAIN

Driving up the dirt-road entrance to his home in the dark was a welcome sight for Bloom. His headlights illuminated a tire out front surrounded by kids' toys, easing his blood pressure from the day's events. That was until he noticed the Fiat parked next to Rachael's truck. The vehicle proudly displayed a large Institute of Mining sticker on its skewed bumper, meaning Preston was already home. He must have wanted to get an early start at making money.

Bloom had not told Rachael about his new jewelry business, anticipating her disapproval. He was planning to get home before Preston and fill her in, but that opportunity was blown now and undoubtedly Preston had blabbed about making a ton of money for basically a weekend of work. Bloom contemplated turning around, but it was too late, she was at the door.

Her short, jet-black hair was blowing backwards around the nape of her graceful neck, her chest out, and a big wooden spoon in her hand. The spoon was beating against her leg, spelling trouble for the man with alcohol on his breath. Bloom popped another breath mint before he left his truck. The welcome home mat never looked so ironic as he crossed the entrance to embrace his loving wife.

"If I wasn't so mad right now, I would be giving you a big kiss, maybe even more. So what gives, Charles James Bloom?"

Rachael always called him Bloom, or Charles, but never used his full name. She was definitely pissed. He kept a few feet away, hoping the mint mixed with the Lotaburger onions would camouflage his drinking.

"I know, you're upset and you have every right to be, but let's just sit down and have a bite. Where are my two wonderful children and Mr. Big Man on Campus?"

"It's almost 8 o'clock! The kids are in bed and Preston went out to check on my sheep. It's been a while since I had a man around to help," retorted Rachael, taking aim at her husband's extended Santa Fe sojourn.

"Rachael, I'm sorry. What do you want me to say?"

"How about you explain why you are hiring Preston for $2,000 dollars and what this new jewelry venture is about?"

Bloom spent the next 40 minutes detailing how, since he had a new backer, there was no risk to his business or to Preston. He did neglect to mention that the backer was FBI Officer Shirley Simplton, and there was an infamous list he was perilously close to being put on. Instead he emphasized how the money would help Preston during his next few months at school and would also diversify Bloom's gallery product line. He pointed out it was not like Rachael was making her expensive sculptures anymore, her time only allowing for at most three rugs a year, so the jewelry made sense.

Rachael prodded him for more details regarding the backer, but Bloom feigned hunger, so for the second time in two hours, he consumed his supper. He ate it all, not wanting questions or problems for the night. After all, he hadn't seen his wife in nearly two weeks and the spoon was still in her apron.

CHAPTER 25

MR. MONEYBAGS

There was no snuggling that night for Bloom. He knew Rachael was angry, but primarily hurt. She expected more from him, a man who always shared big decisions with her, or at least used to.

Valentine's Day morning was more promising. The aroma of cowboy coffee tantalizingly drifted into their bedroom. Bloom was surprised his head hurt. The beers had taken an unexpected toll. He was starting to feel like the 50-year-old he was.

"Where are my kids, I can't wait to see how they've grown," Bloom announced as he walked into the kitchen, hoping for a positive response. It was not forthcoming.

"I took them over to Linda's early this morning while you were sleeping. We need to talk," Rachael replied.

"Sure what's up...."

"What's up? Really? You tell me, Mr. Moneybags."

"Listen, I know you're hot about me not telling you about Preston helping me out, but this all happened so fast. I have a backer who is willing to pay for our expertise in Navajo jewelry. The venture in jewelry is going to be a great addition, not only to the gallery, but it will help local smiths who could use the money. There is no downside. My investor is willing to invest up to $50,000 to buy jewelry and we will split the profits. My part is I have to buy and sell the material."

"$50,000 is huge, Charles Bloom. Are you sure there is no downside? Did you sign papers? Where's the money? Were you given a check or —"

"Come on," Bloom interrupted Rachael's barrage of questions, trying to alleviate her fears. "Listen, it's all good, trust me. You know I'm not going to do something stupid that would potentially hurt our family. I was smart enough to marry you, wasn't I, even if it did take me too long."

Presenting Rachael his best "trust me" smile, hoping this would end the conversation, Bloom drew on his salesmanship in spades.

"OK, Mister," she sighed, "but I want to be kept in the loop. I trust you, of course, you're my husband. But I have two kids to worry about and if you're lucky maybe we can work on number three tonight. After all, it is Valentine's Day." Rachael's loving demeanor was returning. She rubbed her hand along Bloom's back, looking for a positive response.

"Honey, I can't wait till this evening, but let's not spoil it with kid talk. You know I'm still trying to figure out how to be a good father to two kids. Besides, you've got your figure back in fighting shape. You're not ready to give that up again, are you?"

Before Rachael could respond, he suggested, "Let's see how the jewelry business works and if we can make extra money to help support a bigger family. Your mom only had two kids and I'm an only child, so three seems a lot to me. I need a little time."

Rachael's expression went from sexy back to all-business short-order cook. She was hoping for more. Bloom realized he would have to confront his child-bearing fears soon, not to mention buying her a card. He had spaced out on Valentine's Day, not good for a man already in hot water.

Which was when Preston waltzed into the kitchen. "Eggs?" he sniffed. "Fresh eggs and coffee? What's up, Mr. Moneybags?"

Bloom did not like his new moniker. He hoped it wouldn't stick, especially since he was anything but rich.

"Yup, Preston, today's our start. You ready to help me locate some great jewelry? You're on the clock now. All I ask for is a good day's work. We need to cover a lot of ground this weekend, so some days may be longer than others."

"No problem," agreed Preston. "I have already set up appointments with five smiths nearby. All are good, one is great. You got cash? The check stuff won't work here. You know that, right?"

Bloom did know that and had a wad of cash. He had picked up $9,500 from the FBI in Santa Fe. He worried when he signed the unofficial-looking receipt. The terms were vague. In small type it stated, "For procurement of Indian jewelry authorized by Agent Simplton." She gave him a copy with her signature barely legible, assuring him it was fine. It would be provided in increments of $9,500 as needed.

He took a photo with his iPhone of the bundles of $100s in her office when she walked out of the room, scooting her nameplate next to the pile as some sort of evidence, hoping it would hold up in court if anything went bad. It never hurt to try and cover one's ass, especially when one's inner voice was advising, "Run!"

Shirley wanted to meet again in a week, and to be called immediately if any source of fakes appeared. Bloom had felt like a drug dealer or snitch walking out with a wad of cash and a meeting set up for next week.

CHAPTER 26

MAKING THE ROUNDS

First stop on Preston's schedule was the Benally family, great weavers and even better silversmiths. Hastiin Benally spoke little English so Preston translated. It was obvious that the old man knew his way around a forge. Many of his stamps were from his father. His style was more 1940s than contemporary. Bloom, who had no intention of remaining in the jewelry business, was nonetheless intrigued by the workmanship, which was apparent even though he knew little about silver. Preston relayed the prices to Bloom, who shook his head yes or no, and pieces were added to a small pile: three bracelets, two pairs of earrings, and a belt buckle. The total cost was a $1,100 for the group. Bloom remembered Blue's advice and offered him $900. He thought it was fair and was surprised when the old man reached for the group to put them away.

Bloom was taken aback. "Does he think these are hardball tactics?" he asked Preston. "What should I do now?"

Preston looked at Bloom as if he was a child and said, "Pay the man, and do it before he changes his mind."

Bloom eagerly nodded. "OK, tell him we will take them, sorry for the confusion."

Hastiin Benally eyed Bloom and laughed a deep, old man laugh. Then he said to Preston in broken English, as if Bloom were not in the room, "I feel sorry for him, not much good at dealing. I'll make it $1,000 because he's married to Rachael. We Diné need more buyers. Also, all cash."

Benally winked at Bloom. Obviously his understanding was better than he had let on. Bloom's face turned red. He was not sure if it was a joke or an accurate assessment of his negotiating abilities, a skill set he thought he was quite adroit at until getting into the jewelry business.

It turned out it was a bit of both. The old man was in high demand, one of the top silversmiths on the Navajo Reservation. He normally didn't wholesale much but was doing it for Preston and Rachael. The Heard Museum had named him as its artist of the year and he was saving most of his material for the big event that was in a few weeks. What he showed Bloom was all he could spare, and the old man knew that money wasn't going to be much of an issue after the Heard Show. Bloom counted out the hundreds from a little pouch he kept around his neck. Then Hastiin Benally gave the pieces a final polish with his worn rag and placed them in a plastic Ziploc bag, each wrapped in toilet paper, and handed it to Bloom. Bloom asked for a receipt, this time looking directly at Hastiin Benally. Preston translated as before, ignoring the fact that it was unnecessary.

Benally answered Preston in Diné, ignoring Bloom.

Preston relayed, "He says what you need a receipt for if you got his jewelry?"

Bloom explained it was for his records, which Preston translated.

The response was, "What's a record?"

Bloom realized he would need to make detailed notes in case Simplton became suspicion of Bloom's spending habits. He took a photo with his phone of the old man and the package of jewelry. As soon as he left the house, he unwrapped each piece and placed a small piece of paper by it with the price he paid for it, with the backdrop of Benally's hogan. Records were not something required on the reservation, at least not in Benally's world, but the FBI wouldn't be as forgiving.

The next three stops went as scripted. Bloom had Preston fill him in before the appointments as to what he could expect as far as negotiating and it went more like he had planned. He spent a total of $5,500 more and was starting to feel that maybe he could make a go in the jewelry business. No one wanted to provide records so he had gone through the same process as before, taking photographs of the jewelry in front of the silversmiths' homes. This might even work better, especially if he found fakes. No receipts would prompt less suspicion. He purchased a nice variety of pieces, all of them seeming very authentic. Nothing resembled the forgery pieces to his eye.

The last stop of the day took Bloom to a small trailer at the base of Sleeping Mountain, an idyllic location with large, hundred-year-old junipers gracing the property. The trailer was of the eighties variety. A very old wooden hogan was less than 50 yards away. It had been abandoned long ago. Its roof timbers were bowing on the verge of collapse. The trailer's owner was Roscoe Buckeye. Preston had first met Roscoe hanging out at the minimart on 491 at the turn-off to Toadlena when Preston was a young teen. For Preston, Roscoe had seemed the big brother he had never had, helping him to master silverwork. Roscoe had problems with alcohol but when he was clean he was a particularly good smith. Preston told Bloom he had experienced trepidation in setting up the meeting, as he was not sure of Roscoe's current sobriety, but he felt he owed it to Roscoe to have at least a chance at some easy money.

Roscoe met them at the trailer door, opening it before they could knock.

"Hey bro, how's my little college boy doing?"

Bloom could tell Preston was edgy about Roscoe's likely imbibing although he seemed passable.

"I'm doing well. This is my Aunt Rachael's husband, Charles Bloom. He's the guy I told you about. He's looking for jewelry for his Santa Fe gallery, really nice place."

"Great. Think you're going to like what I've got for you, been working hard this year making good jewelry. Got to get me a new truck." Roscoe peered in the direction of his badly damaged Ram pickup. It looked as if it had been in a rollover and it was hard to imagine it could even be drivable.

"Yeah," agreed Bloom. "You're right, looks like you need a new one. So let's see if I can help you get that down payment." Bloom knew he was being pushy by not engaging in small talk but the day had been a long one and he was ready to see his wife and kids, plus he still needed to get that card.

"OK, come into my gallery. I'll show you what I got," Roscoe chuckled at his humble surroundings as he ushered them in.

Preston and Bloom were shown to the couch, a piece of furniture only fit for a porch, and they waited for their host. Bloom guessed Roscoe at about 40, with a shuffling walk.

Roscoe returned with an old blue velvet tray filled with jewelry, all of it nicely displayed. It was quality material.

Bloom knew immediately it was the same thing he had seen at the FBI meeting in Santa Fe: fakes. His heart started to pound. He had found one of the sources. Now he had to play detective. He unobtrusively scanned the room, looking to see if there was anyone else lurking and if he and Preston might be in trouble. The trailer was sparsely furnished, nothing of note. There was one large cracked mirror. As Roscoe bent over, Bloom could see in the mirror that a gun was tucked in the back of Roscoe's pants. Bloom felt a rush of adrenaline and not in a good way. He wasn't cut out to be a spy. He was afraid if he didn't handle the situation correctly, he might be in deep trouble. He looked intently at Roscoe, who plopped down on the couch next to Bloom. How far could he question the forger?

"Nice, huh?" Roscoe said with a crooked smile.

Preston's attention was already elsewhere, texting on his smart phone.

"Looks very nice. Is this all I should look at today?" Bloom figured maybe he could see where Roscoe kept his stash.

"Yep, this stuff took me a while. Really quality. Check out the stones I use, nothing filled here. Just first-grade turquoise from Nevada. Cost plenty."

Bloom picked up the pieces, examining every detail to assure himself these were the fakes, but not taking so long that he would arouse Roscoe's suspicion.

"So how much do you need out of these?" Bloom asked, eyeing the bracelets and already suspecting that they were being pushed to the Navajo at $30 a pop.

"Well since you're Preston's relative, how about $100 a piece? If you take the lot, I'll take off another 10%."

Bloom knew Roscoe was tripling up what he'd paid and selling non-Native jewelry as real. A criminal offense, even for an Indian. Bloom's heart was slowing down as he took his time, trying to keep his forger placated. He needed to pace himself.

"I'm afraid that's too rich for me. I've been to four other smiths today and they about tapped me out. But thanks for showing me. Nice stuff."

Roscoe looked like he was starting to worry. He was into them cheap and he thought he had an easy mark but it was turning out Bloom knew what he was doing.

"OK, let me sharpen my pencil. Maybe I can do better. After all, you're kin now." Roscoe took out a pad and began jotting, acting like he was refiguring all the time and effort he had in the pieces. "How about $60 a bracelet? You can't refuse that."

Bloom knew he had Roscoe and at that point he mainly wanted to see how cheaply Roscoe had bought them. He figured any information regarding the cost would help determine if Roscoe was the first in line of the forgers. "I'll give you $45 each, best I can do," Bloom negotiated.

Roscoe frowned and got up. Bloom watched Roscoe's rear and the gun tucked into it in the mirror, worried he may have overplayed his hand. His heart sped up again.

"Listen, let's split the difference. Say, $50 each. That's half off what I want. You don't want to hurt someone who can make you plenty more good pieces, do you? I'm putting the final touches on a bunch more tomorrow. You can have first crack at them, same price."

Bloom realized he needed to close the deal and get out of the trailer. He was getting in deeper and was afraid someone might be watching his every step.

"OK, deal. I'll take all you've got." Bloom stuck out his hand and gave a very limp Diné handshake.

"I see you know us Navajo. Nice doing business with you," Roscoe nodded.

Preston finally raised his head. "We good? It's been a long day, can't wait to see what Rachael's cooked up."

"Me too, Preston. Me too."

CHAPTER 27

TOO MANY COOKS IN THE KITCHEN

Bloom was missing his kids. He had been back on the rez for almost 24 hours and had yet to see them awake. He was surprised by how much he'd missed his children's faces and the sounds they made. His lifelong pattern of bachelorhood was no more. He loved parenthood, although he did realize Rachael was handling the hard parts.

Now, arriving home to his son's mad race to the door screaming "Dada" made him wonder how he could not want another child? Was it the money? The business portion of his brain thought it would be a financial strain, requiring making lots more art sales in a down economy to feed a family of five. No easy task. The time away from Rachael had been good medicine for rethinking the concept of increasing the brood. His emotional side was warming to the idea even if his left brain was fighting hard to veto the concept. And then his left side pointed something else out. *Hell, I forgot the card.*

Dinner was on the table waiting: homemade biscuits with venison sausage smothered in brown gravy. Mason jars of tea and slices of lemons were perspiring next to the plates, a sign that the food had been there a while. No plate was set for Willy, who was almost 2 years old, as he had already eaten and would soon be off to bed. Sammy's next meal would no doubt occur at 1am.

"Nice of you boys to show up. A little late, aren't we? I'm afraid the food is a bit cold. I was counting on Preston here to give me a hand with the sheep, but no luck with Mr. Moneybags monopolizing your day," Rachael commented in a half-joking tone.

The moneybags moniker appeared to be his new handle for the foreseeable future. He tried changing the subject, knowing Rachael couldn't stay mad very long.

"Preston was very helpful today. Sorry we're late but on the bright side we bought some great jewelry at good prices. Tomorrow I'm going to take the day off and hand Preston off to you, paid in full. Feel free to use him as you see fit."

Preston objected, "What do you mean take off? I've got three appointments set up. We can't just stand them up."

Bloom shrugged, "Is it me or aren't we still on the rez? Just put them off a day. I need to run to Santa Fe and show my partner what I've purchased. Make sure I'm on the right path and get some more *dinero*. Besides, you'll still get paid in full."

"Yeah," Preston reasoned, "but Rachael will make me work."

"That's Rach to you," she chimed in, "and yep, we got some sheep pens to clean out. My fence needs to be mended too and that's just the morning. We begin at 7am."

Preston looked like he wanted to protest further but he knew it was a losing cause and besides he was being well paid for what he used to do for free.

The three ate, laughed, and generally had a great time. Bloom tucked in his children, then finally got to spend some alone time with his wife, whose mood had definitely improved.

"So let's see what you bought today. How much did it cost?" Rachael was in Bloom's college sweatshirt, which was worn out, the letters saying N SU, the "M" having been completed washed away. It was her favorite.

She looked ravishing in it. Bloom's hunger had only been partially filled by biscuits and gravy. "You want to see the jewelry? Can't that wait till the morning? How about seeing my well-sculpted abs instead?" he teased.

"We'll get there, don't worry, but let's start with the goods. You spent almost seven thousand today? You must have done well, so let's see. I like jewelry as much as the next girl, especially Indian jewelry, not to mention it's Valentine's Day."

Bloom froze, remembering he hadn't gotten a card and it looked like Rachael was hoping one of the pieces he had bought could be for her. Bloom took out a well-worn Donald Pliner shoe bag, an artifact of his bachelor days, and pulled out the jewelry, each carefully placed in a small Ziploc bag with the price and artist's name. He laid the contents on the comforter for Rachael's inspection.

"Nice, really nice. You and Preston did well for beginners. You may not know what you're doing yet, but this is good." Rachael systematically, like the perfectionist she was, went through the bags examining the pieces, patting Bloom on the back. When she came to Benally's bag, she said, "Ni-i-ce, I really like these." She held up a pair of dangling earrings near her ear lobes, looking for Bloom's opinion. He knew he was in trouble, trying not to give away jewelry he didn't really own.

He gave a quick smile. "Nice, but maybe too long."

Rachael feigned a pout and moved on.

Bloom was impressed with Rachael's acumen. He had no idea she knew anything about jewelry, much less liked it. She wore very little and had never asked for any, another great trait of the woman he loved. He hoped this lack of materialism would extend to Valentine's Day as well.

She held up one of the fakes and tossed it to Bloom like it was a bad apple. "What's with this piece from Roscoe the rascal?"

Bloom's face felt warm. "What do you mean?" He tossed it right back at her as if it were her turn. Rachel held it in front of his eyes for emphasis and itemized, "The bezel's funny. The stamp work's pan-Indian, not Navajo. Nice, but not Navajo. None of the bracelets from Roscoe are right. Did he say he made them? This is a very nice bracelet, don't get me wrong, I'd love to own it. But don't you sell all Native material?"

Bloom was shocked at how perceptive his wife was. What with her rapid-fire questioning and on-target observations, he wondered why she wasn't running this case. He mustered a response that sounded lame even to him: "So, you don't think this is Navajo-made even though it came from a Navajo, a person you have known for a very long time who is a good silversmith?"

"Yes, that's what I'm saying, and part of the reason I have my doubts besides the obviously oddly done bezel and stamp work, is Roscoe is good but not that good of a craftsman and would have no problem taking advantage of some green *bilagaana* with a wad of cash. Just sayin'."

Bloom had a better sounding board in his bedroom than he'd expected. "So my wife who I would rather be kissing than arguing with, what would you say is the value of this non-Native piece?"

Rachael pondered, "Well, it's got a great stone, nicely done, sterling silver, with good stamp work, which as I said earlier if you didn't hear, is not Navajo. I would think maybe $175 in a store."

"I paid $50 dollars, so even if I sell it on eBay I'll make a profit. We're just fine. So let's turn off the lights, put up the silver, and talk about how I've missed you."

He could see Rachael liked the "missed you" part but she was still stuck on the bracelet. "Bloom, there is something weird here. You got a great bracelet way too cheap, that's represented as Diné, but isn't. I don't get it. Why and how is he selling it for that price? It must be stolen. Roscoe has issues with drinking. I think he may be pawning something illegal off on you. If they're hot, you'll lose money. Not a good way to start off your business and your partner sure isn't going to like that."

Bloom wished he could tell his smarter-than-anyone-else wife what was going on, but for now he was focused on something else. "OK, Rachael, I'll look into it, promise. We're not out much money, worst case scenario. Thank you for your eagle eye. Now let's you and me get back to more important things. Like working on our baby making technique? How about a Bloom full body massage for Valentine's Day?" Smiling his most seductive grin, he gently pushed her back onto the pillows. The jewelry discussion was officially tabled.

What Bloom didn't know was that Rachael wasn't so easily deterred.

CHAPTER 28

PRESIDENTIAL POWER

The President had been holed up at the quarry for six days and his arm was starting to come around. There was no sign of infection and he could take it out of the sling for short periods of time now without too much discomfort.

More importantly, he could hold his Glock steadily without his triceps wanting to give out. The time at the quarry hideout had also given the President plenty of opportunity for replaying the possibilities as to who could have tipped off his would-be assassin and where that person was now. He needed to be ready for another altercation, not caught off-guard like before.

The kid was the logical first choice but somehow didn't make sense. It was obvious he had no clue about the value of his own bracelet's stone, much less what the President was up to. The contact info was somewhere in his home in Gallup, a place that was still off limits. There was something about the kid he just needed to remember.

It came to him on February 15, the morning they loaded up the truck and left the quarry, needing groceries and time back in the real world. The half of the hundred-dollar bill! It was still tucked into the President's billfold. He had promised the kid the other half if he found more turquoise. He fished out his wallet and handed it to PC as he drove. She found the torn bill and read it out loud: "Yellowhorse half to pay on delivery."

That's it, he did have the kid's name! Yellowhorse. Bear Clan. He was sure of that now. "PC, we're heading to Toadlena," he announced, heading his truck for Highway 491 northbound. They left PC's vehicle at the quarry. It wouldn't take much searching to find a family member. He would locate the kid and see what his reaction was when he showed up with the other half of the hundred-dollar bill. After all, he did owe him the other half as he had found the turquoise. Once he located him, the kid would be easy enough to read. If he tried to hide his guilt then the President would be forced to make him talk. Otherwise he might have some lead that would point the President in the right direction.

An hour later, while filling up the truck at the minimart at 491's turnoff to Toadlena, the President got an unexpected and disturbing call from Leroy.

"Leroy, what's up? You ready to sell already?" He was surprised Leroy was selling so fast. He must really need the money.

"No, not yet, although it sure is tempting. What I wanted to let you know was that Blue and Pack came by looking for you yesterday morning. I haven't been able to get ahold of you till now."

There had been no phone service at the quarry so the President had turned his phone off.

Leroy continued, "Pack was very interested in your whereabouts. Asked what you was up to. He said he heard you might have a new find. I tried to shake them off the scent, telling 'em a tale about you finding Jesus, which is why you're out of the loop, but they could tell I was full of shit. Just not good at lying. Pretty lame story too, sorry about that. I didn't tell them anything but I'm pretty sure they knew. Figured you should know, just in case."

The President considered his options, but realized it would be too dangerous to go back to Gallup. They were probably hitting all the trading posts trying to track him down. He knew both men well. Blue was cool for the most part, but Pack could be trouble, what with his obsession about his legacy, that damned walking turquoise museum. Pack wouldn't quit till he found out the truth and it was just a matter of time before Leroy cracked and showed him the stone, if he hadn't already. Pack would try and find the claim, too. Blue was more likely to want first in line to purchase some stones, ground floor, so to speak.

"What do you think's going be their next move?" the President asked.

"I'm pretty sure Pack's going to keep looking for you. He also seems to be picking out jewelry for some big new client. Blue is helping a gallery guy named Bloom get into the jewelry business. He has some fancy store on Canyon Road. Pack let it slip that he was their main source for inventory. Couldn't tell if this was true or not. Pack's heading north. Going to hit all the stores along the way, looking for jewelry for this Bloom character, at least that's what I'd guess. If he gets wind of you, he'll forget jewelry buying and head directly to find you. Best keep your tracks covered."

"That's good information, Leroy. You keep it coming," instructed the President. "I'm upping your carat buyback program to $450 a carat. That just got you an extra $50 bucks per carat."

After the phone call, the President knew that his claim was now in even greater jeopardy, which made finding the kid that much more important. He halfway wanted to find Pack and steer him to the #35 grounds to look for more rock just so Pack would get his head shot off and that might take care of that problem, especially if he was there in the background to take out the shooter. If Pack didn't leave him alone that scenario might get staged yet. The President would see to it that Pack would get his precious #35, but it might cost him his life.

❋ ❋ ❋ ❋

Leroy hung up the phone excited about the extra cash. He would sell the President his stone soon. What he hadn't shared was that he'd been unable to contain himself from showing Blue and Pack his #35 gem-quality cabochon. He was so proud of his work and the importance of the stone, he couldn't help himself. He had known both men so long, and they had promised to keep it to themselves. It was a dumb ass thing to do. He knew it was stupid and if the President found out he would be furious, but it's rare when a lapidary man gets to brag.

It had been 24 hours since Leroy showed Pack and Blue the great cab and Leroy was in deep contemplation as to why he did such an idiotic thing. *I wanted to be the big honcho, just couldn't help myself, could I.*

Even as he beat himself up, he knew exactly why he had done it, for a small slice of recognition in the annals of great turquoise finds. To leave his mark. It was the greatest turquoise nugget he'd ever seen and he had cut it exquisitely. It would always be the first #35 stone cut and when more of the great rocks hit the market, he would forever be associated with that find in the lore of stone men. He'd secured his place by showing it to Blue and Pack, men who knew everything about turquoise.

Leroy had expected praise and admiration from the stone men but hadn't counted on the strong reaction he got from Pack. Pack went crazy over the cab. He wanted to know everything about it: where he got it, how long he had it, if there was more where it came from. When Leroy had demurred, Pack tried to buy the stone, starting at $750 for the rock and finally giving up at $1,100. After Leroy rebuffed all his advances, Pack lit out in a storm of curse words. Leroy had done himself no favors by saying he'd already been offered more and promised a first right of refusal. That didn't sit well with the Pack Man. The price for the rock was way beyond what Pack could afford. Pack would need to do some serious horse trading if he hoped to obtain one of the elusive stones.

Pack and Leroy had been friends for 40 years and Pack had to know there was no way that Leroy would do cash and trade for something so special as #35. Pack would have to find the President and take it up with him. Leroy was glad he had warned the President, even if he didn't let him know the full story.

Blue, on the other hand, had reacted in a more muted manner. His take on the stone seemed to be the opposite of Pack's. Blue didn't have much to say about it. Maybe he was not as savvy about stones as Leroy thought, or more likely Blue was simply playing it cool so as not to let on how much he wanted to get into the action. Blue had watched Pack's reaction and had tempered his own.

Leroy decided he would keep the stone in a pouch around his neck for safe keeping. He wouldn't take it off. As soon as the President got back into town, he would cash out, which would keep him from doing anything stupid again.

Yet poor Leroy's pride was going to prove his downfall. He would soon receive a visitor, a man who didn't take no for an answer. Leroy would never sell his #35 stone and his wife would never know Leroy was initially two names.

CHAPTER 29

BACK TO SANTA FE

Early on February 15, Bloom left a message for FBI Agent Simplton on her cell as he headed out of Toadlena on his way to Santa Fe with all the bracelets, including the fakes he had gotten from Roscoe. His mission was starting to feel even more cloak-and-dagger. The sooner he was finished with the ruse, the better. He could envision Rachael wanting to meet his so-called partner, the bombshell Simplton, and then the marriage might be in real trouble. Hopefully he could hand off the jewelry today with the bad guy fingered, and get on with his life.

Maybe Shirley wouldn't call back at all and he could just leave the stuff at her office and bolt.

No such luck. His cell rang as he was driving past Grants on I-40. It startled him from his thoughts.

"Bloom, you called. What's up? Give it to me," Simplton said as she chomped on a mid-morning snack.

"I've found a source. I've purchased some fake bracelets along with some good jewelry—"

Simplton cut him off in a staccato burst. "Great, great, you could just FedEx the stuff and get back out in the field. I need all the sources. There's too much stuff being made for just one or two guys to fence. Did this guy have a lot or a little product?" Her impatience was made worse by the poor reception and the smacking of her gums.

"I bought what he had. Half a dozen at $50 apiece."

Simplton launched into a stream of consciousness reply. "OK, this could maybe be a primary. Maybe one step away from the head honcho. Good, good. What did he ask for? Just $50 apiece or did you negotiate him down?"

"Started at $100, but we settled on $50."

"I'm impressed, Charlie Bloom, you did good. Valuable info. Anything else you learned?"

Bloom hated the "Charlie" part and he didn't like how friendly she sounded when she said it, either, but decided to ignore it. "He had a gun in the back of his trousers. I've never known a Navajo who was packing. Maybe a gun in a drawer or on a rack, but tucked in, hidden like? That's not something I'm equipped to deal with, no matter what your cop records say."

"Hmm. Sounds like I may need to go over and take a looksee myself. You get over here pronto and we'll talk. Meet me at the office then I'll lay out a plan. Got some more spending money for you, too."

Charles had an uneasy feeling in his gut, like when a deal was about to go south, except instead of a piece of art it was his safety in jeopardy and maybe his marriage. But he was in too deep to pull out.

He made good time on I-40 eastbound, then zipped up I-25 to Santa Fe, finding a parking spot directly in front of the FBI building downtown. A good sign, he thought. After all, it was Santa Fe and empty parking spaces were never a given, especially when the Legislature was in session as it was every February.

Finding Shirley's office was easier this time. He knocked tentatively on the closed door.

"Get in here, Bloom." Shirley wasted no time getting down to business. "OK, let's see the goods."

Bloom plunked the Donald Pliner shoe bag on Simplton's metal office desk with an audible clunk. He pulled out the Ziploc bags filled with jewelry from the individual vendors, lining them up in a row that chronologically represented where the goods were purchased.

"I bought a bag from each of five silversmiths, all in close proximity to Toadlena. These are in order of how I purchased them, starting in the morning. The smiths' names and information are in each bag. I also have a photo I took of each house once I left their residences, if you need it. No one would give me receipts, but I did the best I could to document my purchases. I spent almost $7,000."

Ignoring Bloom's careful descriptions, Simplton adorned her hands with plastic surgical gloves and tore into each of the bags, sorting through the goods quickly. Coming to Roscoe's bag, she adroitly picked out the fakes. Examining them carefully, she compared them to a reproduction she already had. "Yep, dead ringer, no doubt. We got our first live connection. That's great. You touch this stuff after you bought it?"

"Well, yes, when I was sorting them to put them into the individual bags."

Simplton made a pouting face of disgust. "You knew they were fake. At that point you should have tried to handle them as little as possible. Anyone else handle my evidence besides you?"

Bloom knew Rachael had, and paused to figure out the most diplomatic way to give Simplton that unpleasant information.

"OK, who else?" she sighed.

"Well, my wife Rachael examined a few of the pieces. Not all."

Simplton's pout transformed into a scowl. "Why would your wife be touching my jewelry in an FBI operation? Can you explain this to me? This would be the same wife that I distinctly told you not to discuss any Bureau business with? How much did you say?"

Bloom was beginning to despise Simplton and wanted to tell her to kiss off, but she also scared him. "Listen, I'm doing my best here. I tried to document everything professionally. I haven't told Rachael anything, which does not sit well with me. I don't like keeping secrets from her. I had to float this cock-and-bull story about me getting into the jewelry business, and she wants to see what I'm buying as she figures it's her money, too. By the way, she picked these out as being fakes in about a nanosecond, so I'm not sure how big a rip-off deal this really is. She's not a jeweler and she knew right away they're not right."

Simplton stood up from the desk, planted her hands on it, and leaned forward, making her five-foot-two frame as imposing as possible. Bloom figured she wasn't used to being talked to in a condescending fashion and didn't like it.

"Listen here, Charlie Bloom. You are part of an active FBI investigation. You have skin in this game, like it or not, and it's my intention not to get your wife's skin involved too if I can help it. It's partially my fault for not explaining that one should never handle the evidence more than necessary. We always trace for fingerprints and residues. Having said that, you need to get your head on straight. I expect you to cooperate and help me break this case wide open. With regards to your wife's expertise in spotting the fakes, well quite frankly I think it's pretty remarkable. Sorry she's not my primary operative but unfortunately I'm stuck with you." With this, Shirley sat back down in her seat and swiveled away to look out the slice of her basement window that provided a view upward to a group of leafless elm trees, their branches blowing in the late winter wind.

After thinking about the next step, she turned her chair swiftly around. "I need you to go back and push this Roscoe guy for more information. Tell him you need lots of material just like this and you will pay him $60 a bracelet this time. Hell, you can tell him $100. The point is, you need lots more. Let him know that you know they're fakes, but that you don't give a shit. We need the primary source. This guy is a lower operative but still he is a connection, the only one we have that's alive." Simplton leaned forward across the desk to catch Bloom's hand, gripping it as an angry lover might, just tight enough to be uncomfortable. "So can you do this for me?"

Bloom just nodded, a rare loss of words on his part, though he did have a couple in his mind he wished he could have said out loud.

CHAPTER 30

CORPORATE HEADQUARTERS

Cambridge Xanadu International, CXI for short, was a conglomerate of subsidiaries whose primary focus was mining. Its holdings included limited resource commodities, silver, gold, and rare earth metals.

Corporate headquarters were located in the heart of Johannesburg, South Africa, in the CXI building complex. Its main tower was one of the tallest structures in all of South Africa. It was built in tandem with the Soccer City Complex in 2009. Known by locals as the Calabash for its gourd shape, the stadium was a thing of beauty. CXI CEO and founder Retieff Hearten, a huge soccer fan and partial owner of the Soweto Suns soccer team, had decided to build the 75-story structure not because he needed a new corporate tower, but so he would be able to view his favorite sport. The extravagant spending was not unexpected from a man who spared no expense on things he wanted. He was used to getting his way, regardless of the obstacles. Laws were only abided if they helped his cause. Hearten's few close friends called him Reff. A fitting name, as he was the man in charge of all outcomes.

His enemies had a less kind nickname for him: Black Heart, one he had earned. Hearten once was one of the biggest supporters of apartheid. Those who went against him had a bad habit of disappearing or when they did show up it was in pieces, minus the heart, his trademark. When it became apparent to Retieff Hearten that Nelson Mandela would command the country and apartheid was doomed, he switched alliances overnight and took care of many of his old friends in the name of solidarity and of course company profits and survival. CXI had grown substantially by hedging its political bets as well as ridding itself of competitors.

CXI was now one of the largest mine operators in all of South Africa and had been aggressively branching out across numerous continents in search of new mineral deposits. Currently it had interests in all but two continents.

A small mining operation was being established in the southwestern United States, where CXI was developing a tract of high-grade turquoise. The mine had been operational for nearly a year. The turquoise was a decent commodity that filled a niche. The true interest lay underneath the turquoise, however, in a substantial uranium deposit, uranium deposits being numerous in New Mexico. The turquoise was a bonus but the goal was uranium. So CXI had been mining the raw turquoise. Once all the turquoise played out, there would be a mother lode of uranium waiting to be removed.

It wasn't until one of his large competitors presented a substantial offer to buy the obscure mine that Reff become suspicious. CXI had been selling the unprocessed turquoise to a company that made knock-off jewelry using the turquoise to create Navajo-style jewelry that then got sent back to the States. This use seemed reasonable to Reff. The stones were staying in the States more or less and he wasn't a big fan of the Navajos who had petitioned the New Mexico governor to stop CXI from digging so close to known areas of uranium because of possible contamination of ground water. As was his modus operandi in South Africa, Reff had managed to buy off one of the key local Navajo officials who for now was keeping things in check.

Then came the unexpected offer from a Taiwanese group that really got Reff interested in the small-time operation. The offer was too aggressive a bid for just uranium and turquoise. Something else must have been a motive.

It turned out that a Chinese company was using the Taiwanese company as its shell. The company, Europa Earth, had bought the Taiwanese company to make clandestine deals, making them harder to track. Europa Earth was CXI's largest competitor. It was the leading mining operation in the world in rare essential metals. Reff smelled a rat, and it was living in China.

After some additional digging, literally, the CXI geology team found what they were after, the reason why the Chinese corporation was making its offers. It was iridium, an extremely rare and valuable metal. It turned out that the company making the turquoise into fake Indian jewelry was also owned by a subsidiary of Europa Earth. Like all minerals they purchased, they tested it and found trace amounts of iridium mixed in with the raw turquoise rock. They concluded that somewhere underneath must be a larger vein of iridium. It didn't take much of this stuff to make a lot of money.

The offer to buy was turned down and CXI turned up the heat at its Crownpoint plant. It was now an iridium mine and anything that got in the way of that would not be tolerated.

CHAPTER 31

MAX THE KNIFE

Max Solenhosen had been handpicked by Reff as head of operations 15 years ago. Reff had observed Max's ascent since he was a boy. Max's father, Otis Solenhosen, a German expatriate, had fled Germany at the end of World War II. Reff, whose own parents had left the homeland after World War I, was always open to those with ties to the old country.

In Germany, Otis had been an SS officer attached to Dachau. He was only 22 but mature for his age, and was put in charge of road construction around the concentration camp. Otis was a bull of a man and feared by all his captives, not to mention many of his fellow officers. He was notorious for working his prisoners to the edge of death. He had little tolerance for those who did not work hard and hated the "inferiors," as he called them, the occupants of the camp. In 1945 the Americans freed Dachau and Otis escaped. He blended in using prisoners' clothes covered in pig feces. No one wanted to get too close to the foul-smelling prisoner. He acted as if he were dumb, until his opportunity arose to slip away one night. He made his way out of Germany and ended up in South Africa three months later, arriving well dressed and with $500 in gold coins. It was unclear how he came to possess so much money, but it undoubtedly required foul play.

Otis, who was very bright, built a successful business in construction using many of the same techniques he had plied in Dachau but to a lesser extreme, employing poor South African workers. At 45 and financially secure, Otis took the time to marry a South African woman of German descent who spoke perfect German. She bore him two children. Max was the youngest, born in 1975. Otis adored his son and hoped he would follow in his footsteps, which he did.

Max went into the Army Special Ops division when he turned 19. He excelled, just as his father had. He received his moniker Max the Knife during an undercover operation in which he singlehandedly killed five heavily armed men using a Spetsnaz Ballistic Knife, his weapon of choice. Max continued to gain notoriety in South African Special Forces and would have stayed in the Army for life if it hadn't been for Reff, who saw great potential in Max's mix of a superior intelligence paired with a Special Forces skill set.

Max was sent to college to get a degree in geology, which he easily mastered. With a good education under his belt, Max could understand the nuts and bolts of CXI's activities along with the bonus of his steely demeanor and lethal capacities.

Now, after 15 years at CXI, 39-year-old Max had autonomy in the corporation. He was Reff's lieutenant and trusted completely. Max would go to trouble spots and take care of problems in whatever method seemed most appropriate. There was guidance from Reff but nothing ever in writing or through telecommunication. The chairman was always insulated. That was policy and Max understood his role.

The two would meet in a special room in the main tower headquarters, where they would talk and watch soccer while laying out the goals for resolving the special problems of a particular hotspot. Max would suggest to Reff a number of scenarios for fixing the problem, then a plan of action would be determined and Max was off until the problem was taken care of or the plan needed to be revised. Sometimes these assignments could require a year or more of legwork.

It was not known exactly how many problem individuals Max had fixed for the corporation over his 15 years. The CIA had followed his activities as closely as it could. The working number was 20 kills, though nothing tangible had ever been confirmed. The actual numbers could be higher, much higher. People disappeared and problems got solved. In third world countries this was not unusual.

Max loved his job and was a force to be reckoned with, traveling the world with power and freedom to do as he saw fit. For over a year now, Max had been assigned to Socorro, New Mexico, working undercover at the NM Institute of Mining and Technology at a CXI-sponsored building which was supposed to be for research in mining but was actually a ruse, using the university as a cover. Core samples had confirmed iridium. Small amounts of iridium were being mined and processed through the university as a clandestine research project of rare earth metals. It was difficult to gear up to the levels needed to make the mine a major player, but that problem was in the process of being rectified. That was Max's job.

CHAPTER 32

BLUE GEMS POINT THE WAY

The President and PC strolled into the Highway 491 quickie mart not long after his conversation with Leroy. There was a small flea market of locals across the street selling used clothes, baked breads, and local arts and crafts. Perfect. The President observed the haphazard vendors set up for locals.

It was cold outside with few visitors but they were hoping to catch the President's Day weekend holiday traffic. The six-foot-two Anglo with long grey hair, a sling, and his much younger Anglo girlfriend tagging along, stuck out as they strolled through the sea of dark faces, although the rez was a place where the President felt at ease.

He was looking for leads but ended up buying a new bracelet with a recycled piece of Cerrillos turquoise. Finding material to sell wasn't his goal, but somehow it always found him. Today's find would only require popping out the cabochon and melting the silver, which would triple his money lickety-split. The purchase also opened the lines of communication.

"Thanks for the bracelet. I'm looking for some more pieces with nice stones. I know a kid that's Bear Clan, named Yellowhorse, used to live around these parts. I think he's in college, maybe U of A? A real good silversmith. You heard of him?"

"Oh sure, that's Rachael's kid, Preston. He used to go to U of A but transferred to Socorro. He's a nice kid and he's got some good stuff. Not very traditional though. I can get you more like mine if you want classic stuff?"

Bingo. It was that easy. The President gave the jeweler his best "I'm a good guy" smile. "Yeah, that sounds great, but I would really like to talk to Preston. Have you seen him or maybe you can point me in his mom's direction?"

"Yeah, he's around. Supposed to be working with Rachael's husband Bloom. I hear they're buying jewelry for Bloom's store in Santa Fe, spending plenty too. If you want more bracelets like the one I just sold you, better get some while I still got 'em, before Bloom and Preston get here. I heard they bought all of Roscoe's stuff yesterday and Roscoe said they're coming to see him again tomorrow. So what do you say, you want to get something else while it's wholesale?"

The President patiently glanced at the remaining pieces, all of which contained poor stones. He had already snagged the best. Then he saw what hid under the cuff of the heavyset old man's red down jacket. "What's that you got on there, anything you want to sell?" he pointed, honing in on a large fifties bracelet with even larger blue gem stones.

"Oh I don't know, this was my dad's piece. It's worth a lot of money."

"How much?"

The jeweler scoffed, "$1,000. Can't get stones like this no more."

"You're right about that. I'll take it." The President didn't want the jeweler having any second thoughts. The jeweler handed the bracelet over to the President who slid it onto his good left wrist. A dead fit. He might keep this for himself for a while. He pulled a wad of hundred-dollar bills out of his roll and counted them out, the cold hurting his fingers.

The old silversmith smiled, revealing he had no front teeth. It was turning into a good President's Day weekend for him after all, the President figured. "So how about you draw me a map to Rachael's house and Roscoe's? I would like to see what jewelry Preston and Roscoe might have," the President asked.

"You got it, Mister. When you see Preston, tell him hi. My son knew his dad. Our families go way back. You going there today?"

"Not sure, I'm heading up to Shiprock today but I'll get there soon," the President responded casually. "I'll tell him hi. What's your name?"

"Jerry Tsosie."

"OK Jerry, I'll make sure to tell him." The President smiled as Jerry sketched the maps. The President would use Jerry Tsosie as his introduction to Roscoe.

Losing no time, a Presidential decision was made. The President would hotfoot it over to Roscoe first and see why Preston was buying jewelry, before confronting the kid to see if their stories lined up. Any information might help the President figure out what Yellowhorse's motives were in giving up the mine's location to somebody else, assuming the kid had.

The President left PC at the minimart to read her Kindle and get some lunch. He wasn't sure what to expect so on the off chance that there was trouble he slipped her $1,500 so she could shop and take care of herself, and told her he would be back in three hours, no later. Roscoe's place was not too far. PC wasn't thrilled about being stranded but also knew that he was trying in his own way to protect her.

Bumping along the rez roads to reach the old trailer at the mesa took 30 minutes longer than expected. Tsosie's crude map showed the first dirt road on the right, which turned out not to be a road but a cow trail leading to a windmill. It died out after four miles of rough going. There were dozens of low mounds that were obviously Anasazi ruins. When he finally realized he had screwed up, he got out to take a leak before negotiating the grueling rough pasture back to the main road. There were hundreds of pottery shards and arrowheads on the ground, strewn everywhere. It was exciting even for a well-seasoned stone man like the President. He wondered how many thousands of turquoise beads must be scattered among the ant beds that cropped up as far as the eye could see. As the President backtracked, he noticed the land had a beauty to its structure and reeked of geologic wonders. Yet those were distractions.

Taking the next road proved more fruitful. The President finally found the trailer as promised. Out in front with a bottle of whiskey stood Roscoe himself, half lit. Not a good sign for a sunny afternoon. The President's experience was that whiskey and Navajos didn't mix well. It was anybody's guess as to the mood of the man who currently was leaning against a very damaged Ram Charger. The President checked his gun, which was in his holster deep inside his sling. He was glad he had left PC at the minimart. If something did go down, he didn't need a witness and this way she would be innocent if the law ever got involved.

"Yá át ééh," the President greeted Roscoe, trying to sound as Navajo-savvy as possible.

"Yá át ééh. What you want here, man? Looking to buy some jewelry?"

It was apparent by the way the truck was supporting Roscoe that he was in no shape to be trading.

"Yeah, Jerry Tsosie told me you had some good stuff. I just bought two nice bracelets from him but I'm still looking for more. I resale them. Looking for good stones, too. Heard you might be the man." The President wanted to ease into his Yellowhorse questions. He would see what came out of the inebriated silversmith.

"That's a nice bracelet you got on, but I've got the best and low prices too. Just sold some nice pieces to a gallery guy from Santa Fe, so you know it's good."

Ah, an opportunity opened for the President. "Yes I heard Preston Yellowhorse and Bloom came around. What all did they buy?"

"You know Preston? He's my bud, really like that kid. His dad was a cool cat, too." Almost falling, Roscoe plopped down on the sideboard of the truck.

"Yes, Preston's a cool kid. Good silversmith, too. So what's he up to, buying jewelry? I thought he was in school and was a smith himself, not a dealer?"

"Uh huh, he is in school, but helping Rachael's husband get into the jewelry business. Buying a bunch of stuff. I've got more if you're interested?"

"I am, let's see what you've got. Maybe I could see something similar to what Bloom bought?"

"Sure, I got more." Roscoe stumbled to his feet, nearly falling. A .38 revolver was tucked into his pants. The President wiggled his good hand in his sling and pulled his own gun closer and unlatched the leather strap holding it. He would be ready if some shit came down. Buying jewelry from an unknown drunk who was packing was a dicey proposition.

Roscoe opened a metal box that had been delivered to him the night before and laid it out on the back tailgate of the truck. Inside was a large leather bag filled with bracelets. He picked up the bag and placed it on the driver's seat to extract its contents. He placed his half- empty Jack Daniels bottle in an oversized cup holder on the truck floor, leaned himself against the seat, and motioned to the President to come over for a look.

"Here you go, check these babies out. I tell you what, you can have them for $60 apiece. If you buy the whole bag, I'll give 'em to you for $50 each." Roscoe was apparently too drunk to do much negotiating.

The President tilted his cowboy hat back to study the bracelets. Very good stones. The turquoise cabochons were almost worth the price, not to mention the silver. The bracelets had to cost close to $60 each just in materials alone. It didn't add up. The President watched Roscoe closely, wondering if he was being set up. "So I can have all these in the bag for $50 each? Seems like you would lose money on these great stones. Where'd you get the turquoise?" He was eyeing Roscoe intently, just waiting for him to go for his gun. He knew he could easily outmaneuver the drunk if he needed to, bad arm or not.

"OK, OK," Roscoe slurred. "I'll tell you a secret if you don't go telling nobody."

"Promise I won't say a word," the President assured.

"The thing is," Roscoe explained, "I can get plenty more where these came from. I'm still doing fine. You do fine, I do fine, no one loses. It's the best deal ever. I never thought I would be drinking Jack but here I am." Roscoe patted the bottle as if it were his best friend.

The President was trying to figure out what Roscoe was saying, then he understood. "So Roscoe, between you and me, these ain't Navajo, are they? It's cool if they're not. I don't' really give a shit. I like the stones, but be straight with me."

Roscoe grabbed the whiskey bottle for courage and took a long, hard slug of the expensive liquor. "Yep, you figured it out, but don't say a word to nobody. The main man, some foreign dude, don't look like he would play too nice. He wouldn't like it if he knew I said anything to you. I'd get my friend in big trouble. So you want the bag?"

"Yeah, I'll take the bag. Looks to be like 50 bracelets? Say, $2,500? One more thing, what if I want to buy more? Is it possible for me to get more?"

"My friend brings me jewelry if I give him a call. Usually he checks in with me every couple of days. He's a nice guy. I'm sure I can get you a bunch more, you wanna come back in a week." Roscoe's head was starting to slump, drool spilling from the edge of his mouth.

"Sounds good, one week. Let me count out the money. By the way, when are you going to see Bloom again?"

The sound of money being pulled out perked up Roscoe's head. "Bloom called today from Santa Fe. Said he and Preston was going to come back tomorrow morning at 8am. He's gonna be mad I sold all the stuff, but I guess I'll have to get him more next week too."

"How about I leave you five bracelets for this Bloom guy, no need making him mad and him causing trouble. I'll go ahead and pay you the whole $2,500 and next time around you can throw in an extra bracelet or two for free. Why don't you give me your number so I can call you and check to see when you get some more pieces? By the way, your jewelry source, you said he's foreign? How do you know?"

"Speaks funny, some kind of different English, like maybe from that Britain place. I only heard that kind of talk in movies. He don't look like no jewelry guy, neither."

"What do you mean?"

"He's big guy, dressed real nice. Just don't seem like the kind to make jewelry and be selling to Indians. More like somebody you'd see in that Wells Fargo in Shiprock."

"Banker? An educated kind of guy?"

"Yeah, I guess. He seems like a tough, scary guy, well dressed. You don't want to know him, really. Something in his eyes, they don't move, like he can see through you. But don't you worry, old Roscoe will take care of getting the material. Just bring more cash."

"I won't worry, thanks. See you in a week. Nice doing business with you." The President concluded the deal and hustled back to his truck to plan his next move.

Roscoe's story was like something out of a bad movie. A tough British banker distributing fake Navajo jewelry using a drunk Navajo as a fence and incorporating high-grade turquoise, all of it at a loss? The plot seemed ludicrous and he had to wonder if he didn't fit into the equation too, somehow.

As he U-turned and swung away onto the dirt road to pick up PC, the President decided they would spend the night in Farmington. Check into a hotel and have dinner at the nicest place in town. It was good to be back out in the world.

Tomorrow he would wake up early, very early, and be watching when Bloom and Preston showed up. There were questions that needed answers and the President would get them, one way or another.

CHAPTER 33

NO SOUP FOR YOU

After Bloom left for Santa Fe on the morning of February 15, Rachael got busy with one project after another. She only had Preston's sweat equity with the sheep and fencing for one day, and she had to make sure she got as much help from her strapping nephew as possible.

It was already afternoon when she took the baby and toddler over to the trading post to let the owner, now known to the family as Uncle Sal, play with them and babysit. Sal figured cute kids around the post were always good luck for sales, kind of like a cute dog. The patrons hung around longer, thus more sales.

Rachael knew the way to Roscoe's as she had retrieved Preston from Roscoe's trailer on more than one occasion, once when Preston was 14 and inebriated. She had never forgiven Roscoe and doubted she ever would. The fact that now, four years later, Preston and her husband were potentially involved with some of Roscoe's underhanded dealings made her plenty unhappy.

On the drive down the dusty four-mile road to his trailer, a blue Chevy four-by-four truck came flying at her with a *bilagaana* with long grey hair at the wheel. Rachael slowed down, rolled her window up against the blowing dust, and looked in her rear view mirror, noticing the New Mexico plate and a brake light that appeared to be out. You didn't see a lot of *bilagaanas* on reservation back roads, especially coming from what was a dead end. It had to be an acquaintance of Roscoe's, that or an enemy.

Coming into the driveway, her concern level escalated. Roscoe's beat-up Ram truck was immediately apparent, its driver's door wide open with Roscoe slumped over the wheel. Rachael's heart started to race and she glanced in her rear view mirror in case he had been killed and she had just passed the *bilagaana* murderer, but the speeding fellow was long gone.

Carefully, Rachael got out and walked over to Roscoe's limp body. He appeared dead except he was still breathing. The smell of alcohol was apparent as she got closer and then she saw a nearly empty Jack

Daniels bottle lying on the floorboard. Rachael nudged Roscoe's leg with the tip of her narrow-toed boot as one might prod road kill. Then she pushed into his arm with her fist, pressing hard. He came back to life.

"What the fuck?" Roscoe almost fell out on the ground, looking around wildly at who had punched him.

"Roscoe, its Rachael Yellowhorse. You're drunk. Wake up! I need to talk to you."

"Rachael, hey, what are you doing? I just saw your boy and husband yesterday. What do you want?" Roscoe smiled, revealing a large gap where one front tooth was missing.

"I want to know what you're doing, selling fake Indian bracelets to my husband, for starters! And second, you know it's against the law to have liquor on the Navajo Nation and be drunk. What do you have to say for yourself?"

Roscoe surely knew from previous encounters with Rachael that she was not one to cross. She was not above turning him in to the authorities. He was drunk but still coherent.

In Navajo, Roscoe explained he was just helping a friend sell some bracelets for him. As far as he knew, they were Navajo made and definitely not stolen. He said if Bloom wanted to return them, he could, but there was lots of money to be made and nothing illegal going on.

Rachael pressed as to what friend he was helping, but Roscoe would only say he wasn't anybody she knew, not anyone from Toadlena.

"So, you're helping a friend not from here fence fake bracelets."

"I told you Rachael, nothing stolen, all legitimate. Tell Bloom to return them if he wants. In fact, since you're being so damn mean to me, tell him that I don't want no more business from him. He was supposed to come see me tomorrow but tell him to forget it. I'm going to give you back his money and tell him to drop off my bracelets at the Toadlena Trading Post. I'll get them from there." Roscoe fished around in his pocket and pulled a wad of cash. He peeled off three hundred-dollar bills. "He bought six bracelets. Here's your money. Can't do no more business with him, don't need this kind of grief. Tell Preston I'm sorry."

Rachael grabbed the money out of Roscoe's oversized hand, turned, and strode back to her truck. She knew that much cash floating around in Roscoe's pocket could only mean he was doing something illegal.

Once she was in her front seat and about to leave she stuck her head out and with a firm voice chanted in Diné, "Roscoe, the gods are looking at you, the coyote is near. You need to get a blessing ceremony and get off the booze or they will not look upon you kindly. Gods are not to be tested." She then spun out of the driveway.

Rachael was more prophetic than she could imagine.

❋ ❋ ❋ ❋

Meanwhile, Bloom was making the round trip from Toadlena to Santa Fe and back to Toadlena in one day. Black ice just outside of Laguna Pueblo cost him an hour, but he was never so happy to see his welcoming house tire as he was at dusk when he drove into the driveway.

Simplton was coming up from Santa Fe tomorrow to sniff around and get the lay of the land. Bloom figured she wanted to see what kind of person Rachael was that she could discern the fakes so quickly. Bloom was not looking forward to their interaction. Rachael was very intuitive and if Bloom's instincts were right and Simplton was hitting on him, Rachael would pick up on it. She would not like the fact that a bombshell of a woman was honing in on her husband and his business.

But for tonight, just being back home was a relief. As he got out of his truck, he could smell a late afternoon batch of Rachael's famous cowboy coffee brewing intertwined with cooling fresh biscuits. Preston's car was nowhere to be seen and probably wouldn't be until late that night. Opening the door he saw a smile on Rachael's face, a pleasant change of atmosphere.

"So how was Santa Fe? Your partner like what you bought?"

"Yes, she did as a matter of fact." Bloom knew breaking the news about Shirley's visit was going to have to happen sooner or later, but he'd rather wait until tomorrow. At least for the moment Rachael was in a good mood. Why spoil it?

"She? Your big backer is a woman?" Rachael stared at Bloom, waiting for any sign of weakness or guilt.

"Yeah, I thought I told you, she's from the East Coast. Fell in love with Santa Fe and wants to get into a side business and thought jewelry would be a good way. I met her at a SWAIA meeting. You'll like her. She gives me free reign on what to buy."

"What about the fake bracelets? Did you tell her about those? Was she as savvy as I was at spotting them?"

So much for the good mood. Might as well get it over with now. "As a matter of fact she did realize they were fakes, but still liked them as good bracelets for the money. She's planning on coming up here tomorrow to visit some of the smiths."

"Here? Well those bracelets from Roscoe have to go back. I met with him today and he reimbursed your money and said it would be better for you two not to do any more business, which I think is a good idea." Rachael pushed the cash across the dining table at Bloom.

"YOU DID WHAT?" Even as it came out, he knew his screaming was over-reacting. It was not like him to raise his voice at the woman he loved. This was a first. Bloom, who didn't get mad easily, felt his blood pressure skyrocketing as he moved toward her. Rachael had stuck her nose where it wasn't needed and he now had a real problem, one that would get bigger once Simplton arrived.

"Charles James Bloom, you need to step back and lower your voice. I went out to Roscoe to ask him about the fakes. He was drunk as a skunk. Said you should return the bracelets to the trading post and he'll get them. I went ahead and collected your money. You should thank me, not yell at me." She turned her back on him and headed into the kitchen.

Bloom wasn't sure how to handle the situation. He was mad as he ever got but in some ways respected his wife for doing the right thing. However, she didn't know the whole story. Simplton would be livid if she had to return state's evidence. It was not going to happen. Now he had to make this charade right all over again.

"OK, Rachael, let's just drop it. I will deal with Roscoe myself." He picked up the $300 that Rachael had dropped on the table and stuffed it into his shirt pocket.

"Fine and you're welcome."

"The food looks good and I'm sorry I raised my voice." Bloom was looking for a fast exit strategy and hoped an apology would do the trick.

"It did look good, but you can eat it by yourself. I'm not hungry." With that, Rachael went to the bedroom and slammed the door, Preston style, tears rolling down her cheeks as she plunged head first onto their bed, waking Sammy in the process.

Bloom heard Sammy wail. He knew he had screwed up and went in to rock his baby and apologize again, this time like he meant it.

CHAPTER 34

TYING UP LOOSE ENDS

Leroy wasn't the kind of man who second guessed himself, but Pack's anger at being rebuffed was an issue that might have to be dealt with. Guilt was nagging at Leroy. He had screwed up by sharing too much information. What began as a small pebble of regret kept irritating his mental edges until it became too large to ignore. He stopped working to rehash the incident in his mind, then contemplate possible future scenarios. The cold February air venting under the lapidary studio's front door added physical discomfort to his mental anguish.

Yes, Pack was probably heading for the President and this was all Leroy's fault. At least he hadn't sold the stone to Pack, or the President would really be pissed. Leroy had let his ego get the best of him. To be able to say that he, Leroy, had been the man to cut the first cab of #35 and do it spectacularly was a coup he couldn't help but brag about. It was his one shot at fame and he wanted others to know. Yet, telling Pack at this point had been a monumental miscalculation.

Pack's ambitions for his damn museum would get the best of him. Leroy had made a mistake telling Pack he had been offered more money. Trying to be Mr. Big Shot had clouded his judgment. For a split second, Leroy had felt like he was a great stone man. Perhaps Leroy could become the official lapidary cutter of the #35 mine. He alone could cut all of the hardest turquoise stones known to man. It would elevate his position in Gallup from a good stone cutter to that of an artist and smart businessman. If only he could take back his bragging to Pack and Blue.

The knock on the worn mesquite door jarred Leroy's daydreams of greatness and despair. It was a firm repetitive rap, the knock of a confident man.

Leroy's initial response to the sound was fear. He was afraid the President had returned. A shiver of panic shot down Leroy's spine, then eased off just as fast as he realized the President would never knock. He would simply stride in and take care of business. The President's reputation was as a man not to trifle with. He had been good at killing in 'Nam and received metals of valor for doing it.

About half a minute passed. Then a second more insistent rap was heard. No ignoring it. Leroy composed himself and headed for the door, his work hammer still in his hand.

"Hold your horses," Leroy yelled. The small-cleaved cabochon Leroy had been looking at as he contemplated his life was tucked back into its protective leather pouch, securely tied around his neck.

Leroy opened the door and a fresh flow of cold winter air swirled into the studio.

"Hello, Mr. Leroy, I presume. I heard you might be able to help me. May I come in?" A large, muscular man in an expensive overcoat stepped forward.

"Yes, I'm Leroy. Sure, come in, it's too damn cold to stand out here. How can I help you?"

The man effortlessly shut the heavy plank door behind him with a loud thud. "My name is Max Solenhosen. I'm an ardent fan of fine turquoise and I heard you possess such a stone. I'm hoping you might be persuaded to part with it."

Leroy broke out in a noticeable sweat in the cold outer room. Pack must have said something? "I cut stones every day and see a lot of great turquoise. What is it you're looking for, exactly?" Leroy hoped against all odds that it wasn't his #35 cab.

"A dark blue stone, lots of silver inclusions. I think it's being called #35?"

Shit, Leroy thought to himself, *the man knows.*

Max was looking intently into Leroy's eyes the same way the President had. Leroy couldn't lie or he would know. "Oh, yeah, I do have one small piece. But it's spoken for. I couldn't sell it if I wanted to."

"I see. Who is the lucky guy?"

"Oh, I can't say. You know, he might not want it known."

"Wouldn't be Mr. President, would it?"

Leroy looked down at his feet as he repeated, "Really, I couldn't say."

"You mind if I see it? Is it in that little pouch around your neck?"

Leroy raised his head to look at the imposing man, whose grey-blue eyes were staring through him.

"I don't have it with me."

"Really? What's in the pouch, Leroy?"

"Nothing... just some Navajo herbs for protection," Leroy hedged, searching for a response.

"Leroy, I'm afraid you're going to need more than plant material to save you." The man stepped menacingly closer.

Leroy knew he was in trouble and swung wildly with his hammer at his foe, but even with a strong arm from years at an anvil, he was no match for the skill set of Max Solenhosen, who had expected the move.

The athletic Max avoided the hammer's path, the result being Leroy's ill-fated lunge propelled him forward and he lost his balance. Max backhanded him hard. Leroy crumpled onto the unforgiving floor. Max jumped on his prey, his agile feet positioned perfectly, one on Leroy's wrist and the other at the base of his jaw.

"Stop struggling or I will crush your windpipe, do you understand?"

Leroy tried to shake his head yes, relaxing the hand with which he was still gripping the hammer.

"Answer some questions and I will let you go."

Max kicked the ball-peen hammer away, then eased off on Leroy's now purple neck.

Leroy pushed his elbows back and gasped for breath, rubbing at his throat.

"I'll ask you again. Is #35 in your little pouch?"

Leroy shook his head yes.

"Who knows about #35?"

Leroy, struggling to breathe, did his best to answer. "Only three people really know of #35. The President, who brought it to me raw. I cut it for him and he gave me my piece. And two stone men, Blue and Pack. That's all. I swear." Leroy never broke eye contact with his assailant as he spoke. Slowly his breathing returned to a more normal cadence.

Max looked at Leroy for a long moment. "OK, Leroy I believe you. One final question. The President, from what I hear, is not a man you would want to double cross. I'm sure he wouldn't want you telling people about his stone, so why did you?"

Leroy sighed. "Pride, I guess. I was proud of the job I had done cutting that stone. It was the hardest rock I had ever tackled and it came out perfectly. I wanted to share my accomplishment and you're right, the President would not be happy."

Max grinned, hearing the answer. "OK, that's all the questions. I will help you up now." Max put out his oversized, gloved hand in a gesture of forgiveness.

Leroy accepted his offer. Unfortunately for Leroy, the gesture was not made in kindness but as another calculated move on Max's part.

With a graceful motion, Max pulled Leroy up using all his weight as a lever, and then propelled him past his own body. Max grabbed the leather pouch as Leroy went by, spinning Leroy's body like the two of them were performing a dance move. Max twisted the straps on the pouch in a death grip, killing Leroy in a couple of minutes.

Once Leroy stopped struggling, Max released the pouch straps with which he had strangled the stone cutter.

Leroy's limp body hit face-first onto the concrete slab. The sound of crushing facial bone broke the silence of death. A small stream of bright blood pooled almost immediately around Leroy's face.

"Pride, Leroy, is an undesirable emotion in business that can kill you, but I guess you know that now."

Max chuckled as he picked up one of Leroy's bench towels. He sopped up the blood and covered Leroy's damaged head, and then hoisted Leroy's heavy body over his left shoulder. Opening the door to his vehicle, Max tossed the body into the van and covered it with a large canvas cloth.

"The first loose end taken care of," Max muttered as he eased his van down Leroy's dirt road. Like the President, Max was not a man to be trifled with.

CHAPTER 35

NO DEAL

Pack was still brooding over being rebuffed by Leroy when he tried to buy the new #35 turquoise. It wasn't fair. Pack had offered over a month's wages for a stinking four-carat cab. It was bad enough he couldn't have it, but the President apparently had more and larger pieces. Pack was going to make an acquisition for his museum no matter what the cost. It was owed to him, as many times as he had given the President good deals on turquoise on which he always made a bundle.

The way Pack looked at it, his own deal-making days were numbered. Pack sensed that this was his last chance at a great cache. There was no social security for stone men. All he had was his traveling museum. For the President to be so jumpy as to leave town and not show up at the Gem and Mineral Show, it must be a once-in-a-lifetime find, a stone man's dream. Pack was even pissed about the name, #35. He knew damn well that name was a reference to JFK. It was bad protocol to name finds after oneself, even if it was in a roundabout manner. If somehow Pack could find the site and get recognized for the turquoise vein publicly, it might get named after him instead. It would be justice in an unjust world. Pack Blue Turquoise had a nice ring to it.

Pack knew the President was heading north from what Leroy had let on, so it was just a matter of finding his truck or PC's vehicle. PC and Pack were good friends. He was privy to where she kept her spare key. He hoped she wouldn't mind if he let himself in to her house, looking for a clue as to where they had gone.

The house looked like she would return at any moment. Her vehicle was not in the garage, but nothing seemed out of place. Pack spent the rest of the afternoon checking PC's usual haunts, but came up dry. She was with the President, he knew it. PC loved the President, a fact she hadn't ever tried to hide. If the President was laying low, it would make sense that PC would be with him.

Tomorrow, Pack would look for their vehicles north of Gallup. The Navajo rez was big but not very populated. Finding the President would be hard, but not impossible. Pack had numerous contacts and he planned to use them all. Every pawnshop and trading post from Gallup to Shiprock would be called upon. Surely someone would have seen the couple. Pack would tie his search into his jewelry buying trip. Make money and find the President. It was time for Pack to seal a big deal. It was his now or never.

CHAPTER 36

DAYBREAK, FEBRUARY 16

The President not only got up before sunrise on Sunday morning, he got himself out of Farmington and hidden in the rocky fissures of a Navajo hillside before sunrise. He meant business.

He was bundled up and squeezed into a shallow sandstone crevice with good visibility of Roscoe's trailer as the sun cracked over the horizon. His hiding place even shielded him from the biting north wind. The temperature was slightly below freezing with an occasional snow flurry. Looking down from the mesa directly behind Roscoe's trailer, the President had an ideal vantage point to see anyone come or go. His truck was safely out of sight, too, or so he hoped.

His jewelry-buying spree at Roscoe's yesterday had revealed Charles Bloom would make his appearance today at 8am, hopefully with the Yellowhorse kid in tow. The President was here to witness the events. He had already Googled Bloom on his iPhone. There were numerous images of the Santa Fe dealer. There was an old 2011 exposé in *The New York Times* about Bloom helping to capture Willard Yellowhorse's murderer, Willard being Preston's deceased father. He liked what he read of Bloom and hoped the art dealer and the kid were not going to be the source of their own demise.

A dark blue van with Texas plates showed up at the trailer precisely at 8am. The President assumed this would be Bloom, right on schedule. And not a moment too soon, since the President was already stiff from over an hour's wait in the cold. His bad arm throbbed as he watched through his binoculars as a man exited the van. The individual was tall, muscular, and Caucasian, with short blonde hair. He looked to be about 40. Something just didn't feel right. He was in a wool coat, for starters, more urban attire than rez apparel. And that van. The President thought to himself, "Bloom lives on the rez, at least part time. He should have a truck, not a van with Texas plates. The photos on the Internet didn't make him out to be this big and muscular."

The guy entered the trailer. A long five minutes passed. Then suddenly, Roscoe emerged head first, tossed out of his own front door. There was a notable crack and scream, as Roscoe's arm appeared to break on the second metal step. He couldn't hear what Roscoe was saying through his sobs of pain, but it sounded like he was begging, probably for his life. The visitor had a rigid body position and was pointing what appeared to be a Glock at Roscoe. The way the man gripped the gun, using it as a serious threat, spoke volumes about his confidence with a firearm. The man with the blue van ruled the situation. Roscoe was no threat to this man, and both Roscoe and he knew it.

The President watched as Roscoe crawled into the back seat of the van at his visitor's prompting. The man strolled over and hit Roscoe's head with the butt of the gun, and he slumped. The man laid his victim flat and covered him with a grayish colored blanket.

At this moment the President considered taking the bully out himself or at least wounding him. He had the advantage of surprise, one he might not have again. It was a tenuous position, but the President decided he had to have additional information. It would be better to do nothing than to make a fatal mistake. He knew nothing about the man and what business he had with Roscoe. For all he knew, it could be a cop. The guy sure acted like one.

The President figured he would see which direction the van went once it came to the T in the road, then quickly catch up and track them. Shooting a man you know nothing about could be a fatal life decision, but so could not shooting him. It was a tough choice but the President was a man who believed in thinking things out.

Once the van left in a cloud of dust, the President emerged from his hiding hole and climbed up on top of some rocks to get a better view and follow the van's movement. When the van hit the T, it took the north route. This would lead to Shiprock. The President scrambled down, gathered his gear out of the crevice, and just when he was going to hurry over to his truck, a new player showed up. This guy looked more like Charles Bloom, wearing a parka and jeans, and arriving in a pickup truck.

CHAPTER 37

DAMAGE CONTROL

It was Sunday morning on a holiday weekend, usually a day to kick back. Not today. Bloom jolted awake in the pre-dawn light and looked outside. Perfect, only flurries. He knew he needed to smooth out a deal with Roscoe before Simplton arrived and driving to Roscoe's secluded homestead was hard enough without snow.

He checked the weather on his iPhone. His saving grace was an intense winter storm which had apparently just missed the rez but was reportedly a direct hit on Albuquerque and Santa Fe. It was possible it would close La Bajada pass for a few hours, maybe even the day. Simplton would be delayed. Late winter storms in New Mexico can be violent but usually don't last long once the sun comes out.

Bloom decided to let Rachael sleep in, and Preston too, the latter racking up another day of free wages. He figured it was better not to have any witnesses for what he was going to discuss with Roscoe.

He would keep his morning appointment solo. Bloom's plan was to openly acknowledge that Roscoe was selling fakes and that he didn't give a shit. He just wanted the stuff and had the money to pay and keep paying. Rachael's meddling should be overlooked.

Nonetheless, Roscoe packing a pistol was a serious concern. Bloom hoped he was sober today and that Rachael had not been too hard on him. He didn't like his wife visiting drunken men by herself. It was dangerous, even when she knew them or thought she did. Bottom line: Simplton would not be giving back any bracelets today and neither would Bloom.

After showering, Bloom pondered his note for Rachael, eventually settling on: "Sorry again, I'm a fool. Need to talk to Roscoe. Should be back by 10. Kiss our kids for me. P.S. I still owe you a Valentine's gift. I plan on paying in spades. Love, Bloom."

Rachael couldn't stay mad for long and the note might be the extra something needed to find that soft spot in her heart he knew she had for him, even after his yelling and forgetting a Valentine's card.

Driving over to Roscoe's, Bloom squinted against the early morning rays. He rolled into Roscoe's run-down trailer's driveway just a little after 8:20am.

Following good Navajo manners, he waited in his pickup for a couple of minutes before knocking on Roscoe's door. No answer. Bloom hit the metal door harder. He banged so hard, the adjacent windowpane shuddered. Still no response. Peeking into the living room window, he saw no one.

It wasn't like Roscoe lived close to anyone or had a horse. His Ram pickup was still next to the house. It looked in bad shape but probably could run, so where was Roscoe? He had a toilet and electricity, so he didn't need firewood or to go out for water or the john. It was biting cold and not the kind of morning for a walk. Finally, Bloom tried the door handle. It turned and he walked in.

"Roscoe, it's Charles Bloom. You here?" Nada.

Bloom figured wherever Roscoe had gone, he now had a little time to look around. He started in the empty bedroom. The sheets were dirty and what appeared to be a full bag of potato chips was scattered on the floor. It looked like it had been knocked over. The chips crunched underfoot with every step. A pair of well-worn cowboy boots stood next to the bed, otherwise the room was unremarkable. Bloom decided he would go through Roscoe's drawers and see what he might turn up. Just the usual knickknacks—pens, matches, papers, flashlight. Under the bed he found Roscoe's gun, $2,500 dollars in cash, five fake bracelets, and a note with a name on it. This was concerning. Why was this stuff under the bed unless he was hiding it? And why didn't he have his revolver on him? The gun looked like the same one Roscoe had been carrying two days ago. As Bloom's mind began spinning to figure out what all this meant, his heart started to race at the unpleasant possibilities. He began feeling the first signs of panic. Bloom decided he was over his head and need to vamoose, pronto.

He was heading back towards the living room when he heard the front porch step creak. Could it be Roscoe coming back, catching him snooping in his bedroom? Or something worse?

Bloom decided he couldn't take a chance. He dove under the bed and grabbed the revolver, flipping open the cartridge. It was loaded. He shut it and cocked the trigger. The safety was already off. His hands were trembling. His eyes swept over the chips. They weren't knocked over, they had been thrown! That's why the splatter pattern. Roscoe must have thrown them at somebody, and left in a hurry without his boots, money, or gun.

Bloom inched backwards, till he reached the far side of the bed. He steadied his arms on the mattress and pointed the gun at the partially opened bedroom door. Then he waited for whoever was on the porch to come through.

CHAPTER 38

GETTING INTERESTING

Bloom heard footsteps, then the squeak of the front door opening. It sounded like just one person. Objects were picked up then put back down. More shuffling. Somebody was methodically searching the house. Sweat started to run into Bloom's eyes. He wiped his face with his arm and quickly repositioned himself. He wasn't sure if he could actually shoot anyone, and who would he be shooting?

A large figure in a black jacket came down the hall. The hood on the jacket was up. Bloom couldn't recognize the person from his position. The man's hands were in his jacket pockets. He stepped through the doorway. Bloom flattened his body, so only his head, arms, and gun were visible.

"Stop right there, don't move!" Bloom yelled as the hooded giant came through the door.

"What the fuck! That you, Bloom? Thought I recognized your truck. Shit, it's old Blue. Put that damn gun down before you kill someone, and I don't want that someone to be me."

"What are you doing here, Blue? You scared the shit out of me." Bloom lowered the gun, his whole body trembling. He was breathing hard and it was apparent he was more scared then Blue. He wriggled his way out from under the bed.

"I came looking for you. Got done earlier than I thought with my Gallup business, so I figured you might need some help up here. Stopped by the post, then your house, where your missus showed me your note so I scurried up here. I've known Roscoe for a lot of years and he's not a guy I would put a lot of faith in. He's not all bad, but he drinks too much and the deals are always in his favor. Your wife said you was heading to talk to him about some fake bracelets so I figured that was my territory. Saw your truck, came in, then you pointed a gun at me like you were going to shoot me. That pretty well sums it up."

"No, seems like you got some more explaining to do," Bloom disagreed, ignoring Blue's redirect and staying on point. "It took you a long time to get back to this room. What were you doing up front?" Bloom was starting to get his composure back now. Although he was still squatting on the floor, his back against the trailer wall, his mind was clearing. The gun was still firmly in his grasp.

"I was doing what I'm supposed to, looking around seeing if I can find anything of interest for the man, or should I say, woman, in charge. My ass is on the line so I want to get this shit wrapped up."

This seemed reasonable to Bloom. "So, did you find anything? As you can see, Roscoe's not here, and by the looks of the potato chips and mess scattered around the room, he may not have gone of his own accord, thus the gun pointed at you."

"Nah, nothing of interest, just empty bottles of cheap booze. How about you?"

Bloom stuck his head under the bed and retrieved the note. "Besides five fake bracelets, I found this piece of paper. It's got a name, some letters, and something else. Looks like Roscoe was concerned about whoever this is. Look here."

Getting up to show Blue the paper, Bloom avoided touching it except at the corners. "See how it's underlined?" It read: *Max Solenhosen. CXI.* Scrawled underneath the name was a word in block letters: *coyote*. The *coyote* had been traced numerous times, almost like a doodle.

"You think Roscoe thought this guy was a bad spirit?" Bloom pondered.

"Hmm. That's how I see it, but what do I know. You're the one married to an Injun."

Bloom gave Blue a hard look, a fighting look. "That's Indian, or you can use her name if you want, Rachael. But knock off the *Injun* and *squaw* shit if you want me to work with you."

Blue put his hands up. "OK, I-n-d-i-a-n. Like I said, you're the one married to one, so you tell me what it means. If he's got fake bracelets, something's not on the up and up here, that's for sure."

Bloom looked at the scattered chips and closed his eyes, trying to sort everything out. "Roscoe must have felt the coyote spirit. It was a subconscious scribble, I believe. We have to respect that, no matter what we think. I believe Roscoe felt this Max Solenhosen is associated with evil. We need to be careful. First thing, we'll let Simplton know about the note and what's going on around here. She'll be pissed if we touch anything else. I'm expecting her today. I'm going to head back to my house. You want to come and wait with me?"

"I've got a few things to do first. Why don't you let me hold on to the note? I'll meet with you tomorrow and bring it with me. I can take it to a few guys around here and see if they recognize the name or if that's Roscoe's writing. That way you can let Simplton know I'm doing my part."

Bloom, who had already been chewed out once for sharing evidence, disagreed. "I'll give it to Simplton. Nobody's prints are on it now other than the writer's and mine at the corners. It could be important evidence if something has happened to Roscoe. I'll meet you tomorrow and let Simplton know of your efforts."

Blue didn't seem to like that answer. He snapped, "Fine, tomorrow at your house. I'll get there when I can." He turned, not waiting for Bloom's response, and shuffled out the door.

Bloom wondered if Blue suspected where Roscoe might be and if he knew more about the paper's significance than he was sharing. So much for partners.

CHAPTER 39

ALL ROADS LEAD NORTH

The quickie mart on Highway 491 halfway from Gallup north to Shiprock was a natural gathering place. For Pack, it was a great spot for information, one of his favorite places to chase down leads and fill up his gas tank. It turned out that the President had been in just yesterday with a blond-headed girl, no doubt Patsy. The cashier's uncle had sold him a couple of nice bracelets across the road at the flea market and for real money. He was pretty sure they were headed to Shiprock, or at least that was what his uncle had said.

Pack figured if he could find the President, he would be able to pressure him into selling him a #35 cab, otherwise he would blow the find wide open, letting everyone know his secret. If the President was going to Shiprock, it meant he would be staying in Farmington, as there were no hotels in Shiprock. Unless he was hiding out with a friend or in his truck, he would be staying at the best hotel. Pack knew this was the new Holiday Inn Express. It had an indoor pool and was more than Pack could afford, but not the President.

❋ ❋ ❋ ❋

Patsy Clever was spending the day in Farmington by herself. She liked the town and had even considered making it her home at one point, but the President lived in Gallup and no matter how much she tried to write him off as husband material, she still hoped he would come around. She found this city along the San Juan River near the Colorado state line charming in its own offbeat way. Just off the Navajo Reservation, it was a blending of cultures with Navajos, Hispanics, Utes, Apaches, and Caucasians. PC was an adaptable woman who easily flowed with cultures other than her own.

The President had barely slept in their hotel room last night. He had left way before sunup. She had been forced to fend for herself. What else was new? She had gone through most of the snack food they had brought with them.

Today, truck or not, she was getting a real meal and going grocery shopping. There was no timeline on how long they might be in Farmington, so she needed to make the best of it. She had coffee and an omelet downstairs, then planned her day. Their hotel room had a small refrigerator. PC's goal was to fill it. The nearest grocery store was two miles away. Not so bad. It was a cold, gloomy day with snow flurries, but not much accumulation predicted.

The walk to Safeway was longer than she anticipated. Once there, her shopping list was reduced to lighter things not in cans and not liquid. Chips and popcorn headed the list. She considered getting a taxi for her return, if there was one, but figured the exercise would do her good. Besides, it was only 11am and she had time on her hands.

Walking down the main street with shopping bags in hand, just before crossing over the river, PC saw a blue van pull over. A well-dressed white man smiled and offered her a ride. PC had given hitchhikers rides in Gallup often enough and thought she was a good judge of character. The man looked nice enough, and she still had nearly two miles to go.

"OK, I'm not going far, where Bloomfield Avenue comes together with old Bloomfield Avenue, Highway 64," she said, swinging the grocery bags onto the floor and shutting the door.

"You better put on your seat belt. It's the law in this state," the man said with a thick English-sounding accent.

"Sure, no problem. Don't want you to get a ticket. Nice of you to stop for me." She grabbed the belt at her right shoulder, then leaned left to fasten it into its holder and never saw the Taser that hit her squarely in the chest.

She was completely dazed, knocked out in an instant. She could hear but not speak or move. The man finished pulling the seatbelt over PC and clicked it shut. He laid the seat back down, covering her body with the same grey sheet that he used with Roscoe earlier that morning.

If PC had only looked up at the sun visor, she would have never gotten in. Clipped to it was a grainy image of her from her old high-school yearbook. The man was hunting his prey and she had been easy to trap, alive, for now.

※ ※ ※ ※

As fate would have it, the kidnapper was not the only man to notice PC on that bridge. Pack had just driven into town and was driving across the bridge when he sighted PC in his rear view mirror, carrying a load of groceries. By the time he got across the bridge and found a place to make a U turn, a blue van had picked her up and made its own U turn heading back in the direction they both had just come.

Pack sensed something wrong with the scenario. PC was clearly coming from the Safeway. He saw the logo on the bags and she was headed away from the store in the direction of the Holiday Inn Express, exactly where Pack figured she and the President would stay. But now she was headed back towards the Safeway and Shiprock in a van with Texas plates.

It was one of those moments when Pack experienced immediate clarity about the sequence of events. PC had probably been abducted and he had witnessed it. But by whom and why?

He would follow at a safe distant from the van and see how it played out. Tugging his .38 snub nose out of his pack, he laid it on the seat next to him. It looked like it was going to be an interesting day for the man who would do anything for a great stone. Today would test his mettle.

CHAPTER 40

LET IT SNOW

Bloom now held an evidentiary note in what was looking like it could turn into a kidnapping case, maybe worse. He was hoping he had an overactive imagination, but the potato chip splatter looked suspicious. At least he had avoided fouling the evidence this time, picking up the paper by its corners and the jewelry with a Kleenex. He did not want to invoke the wrath of Simplton once more. Bloom deposited his newest clues into his stash of jewelry Ziploc bags and stuck them in the hidden cup holder of his truck for safekeeping.

As soon as he got back home, he would make a call on his landline and let the FBI in on what had gone down. Bloom was starting to get spooked and had visions of his cell phone being traced. He was well aware of NSA tactics, thanks to Eric Snowden, so he figured it would be best to wait. Anyone could be listening in. He would be home in 45 minutes.

How to deal with Rachael was now his top priority. Her potential meeting with Simplton would intensify his troubles dramatically, and now there was the issue of Roscoe's vanishing act. Looking up at the sky, Bloom said a little prayer that the snow was still falling heavily in Santa Fe. If Simplton were delayed a day, it might give him time to figure out a solution. Rachael would not believe the blonde bombshell from Santa Fe was his partner, and if she did believe they were a team, his hesitance to have another child would have her thinking something else might be going on. It was a delicate situation.

Bloom decided to keep the details of Roscoe's disappearance to himself for now. He would just say Roscoe wasn't home.

Rachael didn't waste any time meeting her husband on the front porch, no spoon in hand this time but full of questions. He was hoping to find her at her loom, spinning wool and distracted, but she'd obviously heard his truck pull up through the loose windowpanes.

"So, did that man Blue find you? He seemed odd. Said he was working with you on your jewelry business. Didn't stay five minutes and said he had to go. Is this your Santa Fe partner? I thought it was a girl—"

Bloom interrupted, "Nice to see you too, my love." He put a bear hug on his wife, which he meant with all his heart. "Yes, Blue found me. He's working with me on the jewelry project, too. Kind of a partner, but not the money person. That's the woman I told you about. He's helping me figure out the business and I'm helping him have a Santa Fe gallery for selling some of his own inventory."

"Did you give Roscoe back his jewelry?"

"Not exactly. He wasn't there." The less said on that topic, the better, he figured.

"Well, did you leave the jewelry at the trailer?"

Bloom was stuck. He was going to have to either tell the truth or lie. Not only did he not return the bracelets, he had taken five more that weren't his to take. Shit. But involving Rachael any deeper was only going to put her at risk. "Yes, I left it there."

"OK, that's good, hon. Roscoe's not someone you need to deal with. I'm glad you're done with him. He's the kind that will cause trouble, trust me. He needs a Blessing Way and probably someone to share his life with, if that's possible."

"Rachael, I have no doubt you're right." Bloom was thinking he could use a spiritual tune-up himself, but at least he was lucky in the partner department. "So where's Preston?"

"Earning his keep by cleaning some of last year's wool that I've got stored at the Toadlena Post. He was happy he got to sleep in late, and now he's earning another day's pay for things he used to be expected to do for free," Rachael grinned.

"No kidding," Bloom grinned back at her and slid his arm around her. "Now let's see the kids."

However, there was a threat hanging over their domestic harmony and an observer watching from not far away.

❦ ❦ ❦ ❦

The President had scrutinized Bloom's arrival at Roscoe's. And right behind Bloom, drove in no other than Blue in his crappy green car. Why was Blue working with Bloom? The President didn't know their relationship, but it worried him more than the man with the gun. Somehow Blue was a part of the equation, and for that matter, where was Pack? They had both been looking for him. Pack must not be far behind.

The President had watched. The two men spent about 30 minutes inside Roscoe's trailer, then came out, said nothing and left. They must have been looking for Roscoe or something Roscoe had, maybe the jewelry, or the same thing the man in the van was pursuing.

The immediate question was, who to follow? The President decided Bloom was still his target. Bloom was the key to the Yellowhorse kid, who knew the President was after #35. Roscoe looked to be toast. The President felt bad he couldn't help him, but figured the drunk had probably brought it on himself. The President's immediate concern was his own preservation. The man with the gun was worrisome, but he would have to wait. Luckily, the President had gotten the license plate number of the van. Maybe he could pull in a favor with his buddy that worked at the DMV or turn it in to the police anonymously.

As the President watched, he saw Bloom head south, the same direction he had come from, while Blue headed north, the opposite direction he had come from. The President opted for south.

The President kept his distance from Bloom's vehicle, not wanting to be noticed. He watched Bloom turn in to his home, then he drove his own truck past the home's dirt road as if heading to the Toadlena Trading Post. He turned onto the next dirt road just past the Yellowhorse-Bloom property. There was an old abandoned hogan at the end of the road which the President used as cover for his truck. Using his Walmart binoculars for the second time that morning, he surveyed the house and made himself as comfortable as possible.

The Chuska Mountains loomed close behind him, fresh snow accumulating on the top, though at the President's new location it felt almost balmy now in the late morning, close to forty degrees with occasional broken skies of blue. He thought of his girlfriend PC, stuck in a hotel in Farmington waiting on him. He should call, he knew it, but he was afraid to alarm her.

It was nearing noon when he saw exactly the individual he was looking for: Preston Yellowhorse, arriving back home, probably for lunch. Even from the President's safe distance, it was clear this was the kid who had given him the map. It even looked like Yellowhorse was still wearing the bracelet with the #35 stone. "Hot damn," the President whispered. "Found ya."

There was an easy way or a hard way to try to find out what he needed to know. The President decided that he would try the easy method first. He could always resort to physical pressure if he didn't get the answers he needed.

CHAPTER 41

I PREFER CHOCOLATE

PC's first conscious thought was of the cold chocolate ice cream that had partially melted onto her feet from her now spoiling groceries. Her leg was tingling, the only sensation that was registering. Her hands and legs were bound with duct tape. She was trapped. She glanced over at the driver, who smiled a toothy grin back at her. It wasn't a smile of hello but of "you're mine to do with," an expression she had seen on drunk men before. She was terrified of the possibilities.

"I see you have awakened. If you scream or cause trouble, I will Taser you again, or worse. Do you understand? Nod your head if you do."

PC slowly nodded yes.

"I have been looking for your boyfriend, your Mr. President. He is not an easy man to track down. It was very lucky for me that you were walking down the street, a gift from God, but not as lucky for you, I'm afraid."

"What do you want?" PC asked, her voice slurred and scratchy. She was sure this was a man who could do great harm to her and not blink an eye. She would say or do whatever it took to survive.

"Well, first off, what exactly has your President found? I know he has been looking on Navajo land for some minerals or such?"

"All I know is he found a vein of some super turquoise, very high quality. He's calling it #35. He found one big stone, which he had cut and polished."

"Yes, go on. Where is the stone?"

"He's got some of the cabochons with him, except for the piece he gave Leroy, a stone cutter in Gallup, and one he sold to a guy in Japan. He sent it by FedEx. Put it in a drop box by Walmart in Gallup."

"Japan? Are you sure it was not China?"

"It was Japan. He said the guy was a big Japanese whale who collects turquoise and this was a great specimen to add to his collection."

"Turquoise. Is that all he collects, just turquoise?"

"Yeah, the President is a stone man, deals in turquoise. Nothing else matters to him. Trust me. I know what I'm talking about."

Her abductor seemed to believe that she was telling the truth. "Did he say anything about being shot at?"

"Yes, of course. He was hit in the arm. Nothing bad but he thought someone tried to kill him. Was that someone you?"

"Do you really want to know that? That you might be with a murderer and you're bound up and possibly my next victim? Can you handle the answer?"

PC contemplated this. She knew he was testing what kind of person she was, but hearing it from his mouth might prepare her for what was coming. There was a reason why PC didn't have some house-with-a-white-picket-fence kind of lifestyle. "Yeah, I want to know."

"No, it wasn't me, but I know who it was. If I were you, I wouldn't ask any more questions. Time for you to be quiet."

PC stared out the window, trying to figure out her next move. She studied the topography of the land. It might come in handy. Like the ice cream melting on her feet, she realized she was stuck in a bad situation.

❈ ❈ ❈ ❈

Pack followed the blue van as it left the main Highway 64 west, turning down Navajo-36, a much less traveled road. It was heading southwest towards Morgan Lake and the APS Four Corners Power Plant. Pack followed at a very far distance. The van almost looked like a dot on the horizon, but still traceable. After driving for 20 minutes, the van came to a small dirt road that led to an industrial building, probably part of the power plant's property.

Pack slowly drove by, not stopping but watching until the van disappeared behind the 20-foot metal building. He took the first dirt road afterward, a glorified cow trail, and followed it to a windmill and parked his Ford truck. He was probably a mile from the building complex. Pack couldn't see the van from his angle, but he did have a clear shot of the building and its one window, although with a handgun there was no accuracy. He decided this must be the hideout and he would observe, rather than shoot.

Pack was not hero material. He was more the antihero type, most would say. But he was sure PC was in that van and not by her own accord. The best he could do was some reconnaissance like he and Blue used to conduct in their old Air Force days, and see if he could ascertain PC's predicament.

Following a small wash that ran perpendicular to the buildings, Pack trudged closer to the van. It was hard to get low enough to hide. He had a body that was nearing its end point of usefulness. Coming to a small rise at the last structure between him and the building was as far as Pack dared to risk going. He peeked over the small hill that looked like it was an old Anasazi ruin and tried to absorb the situation. He sniffed an odd aroma of smelting, probably coming from the plant. It was a sickly industrial scent, one that reeked of things bad for one's health. It was strong enough that Pack covered his face to keep from getting queasy.

After about two hours on point, Pack spotted a white man through the one window. He was sharpening a long double-edged knife on a whetting stone. The sounds that came next told the story: a Navajo man chanting. Not a woman's voice, but a man's. Whatever was happening inside was not good. The chant had a desperate sound. Pack had been around Navajos long enough to respect this kind of communication. Whoever was in the building was praying in his own way. "Oh, shut up," the white man yelled, and there was sudden silence.

Pack's antihero kicked in. He hightailed it back to his truck. He had to find the President. He would know what to do.

CHAPTER 42

MY LUCKY DAY

Sitting at the dining table with Preston as Rachael rustled up tacos for lunch, Bloom got a text from Simplton telling him that she was in Gallup heading up 491 and would be there in an hour, maybe less. Damn. Bloom started to panic. He had been counting on the snow impeding her trip west, but now she was almost at his home.

He texted her back: "Meet u at quickie mart at 491 and 19 intersection. Don't have good reception here. I'll be waiting in my truck."

He turned his phone to airplane mode. He didn't want to see the response and he didn't want Simplton to see he had gotten one if she harassed him about it later, or worse, if she was tracking his phone.

"Preston, tell Rachael I have to meet my business partner and I'll be back in an hour or two. I'll eat when I get home, if there's anything left."

"She's gonna be mad you're not telling her yourself. You know that, right? Lunch is almost ready." Preston obviously knew Bloom was up to something, but didn't want to push him too hard even though he was curious.

"I know, just cover for me. I have to go. I'll be back soon. You want to get paid, right? Well this is the individual that pays you."

"Got it. Good luck, you may need it."

Bloom dashed out the door, jumped in his truck, and spun out, heading off the property before Rachael could stop him for a more complete briefing. He was wondering how badly he was screwing up his marriage but he had no choice. He didn't want Simplton to meet Rachael or the gig would be up, and that wasn't even taking into account the Roscoe enigma.

❋ ❋ ❋ ❋

The President watched as Bloom took off. The good-looking Navajo broad stepped onto the house porch directly afterwards, apparently looking for him. Obviously there was some trouble in paradise. She was beating a spoon at her side. Wherever Bloom had headed, it was in a hurry.

This was the President's chance and he seized it. He ran for his truck and headed for the Yellowhorse-Bloom driveway. He was going to confront the kid, pay him the other half of the hundred-dollar bill, and see what he could glean from his reaction. He checked his Glock, made sure the safety was on, put it into his sling and headed for answers.

The President was counting on the surprise factor helping him to get some honest responses, so he coasted down the driveway and rolled to a stop a few hundred feet from the house. He peeked in the window and saw Rachael sitting down to eat with two small kids and Preston Yellowhorse. She startled when he knocked.

Rachael opened the door, but not before flipping a small fastener into an eye hook on the screen door, such being flimsy reservation security.

"*Yá át ééh*, Miss. I'm JFK. I'm trying to track down Mr. Yellowhorse. He helped me find something and I promised if I found it I would give him a reward. Well I found it, so here I am."

"You mean Preston?" Rachael asked, craning her head to see if there was anyone else or if there was a vehicle.

"Yes, Preston Yellowhorse, the silversmith. He helped me find a nice turquoise rock. He told me where to look and I told him I'd give him $100 if I found it. I tore the bill in half and gave him part, so here's the other half." He held up the torn bill as proof.

He knew it was an odd story to say the least, and he couldn't blame Rachael for her wary expression.

"OK, let me find Preston and see what he has to say," she replied, holding up a finger. She didn't close the door, but neither did she unlock the screen.

"Yes, just ask Preston," the President called after her. "He will remember, I have no doubt."

Rachael stepped away from the door and he heard her talking in Diné, no doubt giving Preston the story.

She came back and unlocked the screen-door hook. "Looks like its Preston's lucky day. He's rolling in money. Come on in, JFK. Would you like lunch? We've got extra."

The President figured Rachael was offering him Bloom's portion as punishment for his running off. "Sounds great. Looks like it's a lucky day for me as well."

❋ ❋ ❋ ❋

Bloom got to the quickie mart first, and sat in his truck rehearsing what he would say to Simplton when she arrived. He would tell his story and her response would determine his next step. He hoped she would take the note, let him show her to Roscoe's home, and she would take over from there. If she insisted on going to his house, he would have to tell Rachael the truth about the whole charade. Actually, maybe Simplton should explain it. It'd be better if it came from her mouth, the official FBI version.

The dark, shiny sedan with the tinted windows slowing as it bounced into the uneven parking lot was obviously Simplton's car. It looked like a Fed car. It might as well have said "FBI" on the front plate. Bloom cringed at the thought of all the locals seeing him talking with the bombshell Fed. The gossip would be everywhere. "Shit," he whispered under his breath, realizing he should have met her at the trading post, where at least there would have been fewer people.

Bloom had his window down. Simplton rolled hers down when his car approached.

"This may not be the best place to meet," Bloom told her. "Can you follow me? There's an old sheep pen not far from here where we can talk. I don't need the gossip going around about me talking to a good-looking *bilagaana*. I'm sure you understand. I'm married."

Simplton apparently enjoyed the compliment as much as Bloom hated having said it. It played like he was flirting, which he wasn't, but now he was encouraging her unprofessional behavior with his own poor wording.

"Sure, I'll follow. Didn't realize you thought I was good looking." Simplton winked at him.

Bloom smiled weakly. "Follow me."

The old sheep pen was on Sherman property, Rachael's maternal ancestor's land. Bloom had first met Preston at this very place three years ago when he was trying to find Rachael Yellowhorse. The place held good memories every time he went by. He hoped Simplton wouldn't spoil it for him.

"OK, Charlie," she demanded, stepping out of the sedan and planting her high-heeled boots in the dirt. "Tell me everything and don't leave out any details, no matter how small. By the way, you're not answering your phone."

"Must be off, thanks for letting me know." Bloom regurgitated everything he could remember in the order it happened, and handed over the note and jewelry.

Simplton examined the bracelets thoroughly, then stashed them in her coat pocket. The note she held under the bright New Mexico sun, looking for some hidden message or watermark.

"Take it you didn't touch anything this time, did you?" she smiled at Bloom.

"Correct," Bloom couldn't help but smile back.

"OK, so go over what happened to Blue after you left Roscoe's. Where was he going?"

"Not sure. He said he had some business to take care of and to let you know he was doing his part. He wanted to take the note and show it around, but I told him I needed to give it to you."

"Let me ask you, Charlie, what's your take on our man Blue?"

"Honestly? He's a racist, he's not a fan of authority, and he seems smart, smarter than he lets on."

"Yes, I think you're correct on all accounts. Were you surprised he didn't follow you back to your house? He knew I was coming, right?"

"I guess so. I didn't really think about it. I called him out on some racist term and he didn't like that much. I don't think he and I are the best of friends right now, so it didn't surprise me that he would want to keep his distance."

"Maybe, but he has some fairly significant legal troubles. Seems like he might want to keep the Bureau on his good side, be around when I come to town." Not waiting for a response, Simplton continued, "I'll take my Ford Vic and follow you to Roscoe's. Let me see if it's as dire as you think. Hopefully you've just got an over-active imagination. But if he has been abducted, then we have serious trouble, the kind that even I need back-up for."

Bloom didn't like the sound of this. Simplton did not impress him as someone that got scared easily. He was sorry he hadn't grabbed some of Rachael's biscuits. It was looking like it would be a long afternoon.

CHAPTER 43

WHAT'S THIS HOLE?

Rachael's chicken tacos were excellent but the President's mind was preoccupied with trying to understand what kind of people his hosts were and if they were capable of wanting him killed for money? It seemed to him, a man who always trusted his instincts, that these were not the type of individuals who would set him up.

He watched every facial expression, including Preston's joy when he handed over the half of the hundred-dollar bill. The kid was thrilled. No sign of remorse or concern, just happiness. Seeing Preston's delighted face, he decided he needed to tell the entire story. He started from when he met Preston, continuing until he ended up on their doorstep. He left out the part about Roscoe's abduction for the moment. He needed to gage their response to the rest.

"JFK, tell me—"

"Call me President, Rachael, my friends do."

Rachael smiled a warm but concerned smile. "OK, President, fine, I want to be your friend, too. So you think someone tried to kill you for a turquoise rock, a piece just like Preston's?" Rachael grabbed Preston's wrist, highlighting the bracelet to confirm what she understood to be the crux of the matter.

"Yes, that's what I think. It's a very valuable piece of turquoise and if there's more, it could be worth a lot of money to collectors. The rocks could be valuable enough that someone might kill for the chance to grab the claim."

Rachael seemed to want to understand everything without alienating her uninvited guest and new friend. She reasoned, "Preston here is the only person you can think of who knew you were there, other than the Navajo, Hastiin Begay, who gave you permission to look for the turquoise? After a couple of months hunting, the minute you found what you were looking for, you were shot?"

"Yes, that's the size of it."

"Seems like Hastiin Begay would be more interested in your progress than Preston, wouldn't you say?"

"All I can say is I always listen to my gut. I just don't see Preston or Begay as people who would mean me harm. I treated them both fairly. I paid to be out there looking."

Rachael gave a dubious look that seemed to wonder how fairly he actually had treated them, but she avoided that line of questioning for now, turning to Preston. "You got any ideas, Preston, who else might have known?"

Preston closed his eyes, reflecting over the months that had transpired since he gave the President the lead. "Well now that I think about it, there was one person. You see, I'm a sophomore majoring in geology and environmental sciences at the New Mexico Institute of Mining and Technology in Socorro. There's an older foreign graduate student, Max. He's working on an independent project, heavy metals distillation. Anyway, he noticed my bracelet, too, and thought it was a great piece. I know he liked the stone because when I let him look at the bracelet he seemed more interested in the turquoise than my silversmithing. I figured he's a geologist and so he probably just thought it was a nice rock, like you did."

"Did you tell him about me?"

Preston blushed, which told the President he had.

"Yeah," Preston confirmed. "I guess I did. I told him about the hundred dollars you gave me, and I showed him the half a bill for telling you where I found my stone. I guess I was hoping he might give me a hundred dollars too."

Preston pulled out his wallet and retrieved the well-folded bill. Written on it in blue ink: "The President, pay in full when I find the stones."

The President had forgotten he had written his name on the damn bill. This Max person obviously had seen the President's name and knew where and what he was looking for. "When was this?"

"Right after the semester started in January. Come to think of it, I didn't see Max around much after that. He never spoke about it again and he didn't seem that interested. I figured he was just out in the field doing research, not uncommon for a geology student. He kept to himself even when he was on campus," Preston recalled.

"Do you know what he's working on exactly? Or where he's from?"

"Not exactly, but it did have to do with extracting rare earth metals. I'm pretty sure Max is from South Africa. It's a small school, a few hundred graduate students, maybe. There are a lot of specialists in that field and some of them have a similar accent and know each other. The undergraduate buzz is the South Africans are working on rare earth element extraction. There's even a building dedicated to rare earth minerals. It's funded by some South African corporation, CXI. Lots of high-powered researchers from South Africa in and out of there. Undergraduates aren't allowed in unless escorted. It's off limits without special clearance. I always thought it was kind of cloak-and-dagger, but what do I know, I'm a peon. They give a bunch of grant money to the university, I know that, so I figured it just went hand and hand. You think Max was involved with you being shot?"

"Preston, I don't know what to think, but there's a link from me to you to Max with the bracelet, and my name being on the bill and how to find the turquoise. If we can locate Max, I think we can find some answers. Can I take a look at your bracelet again?"

Preston pulled it off and handed it to the President, who found his omnipresent jewelry loupe in his jacket pocket and studied the rock.

"Preston," the President said, "look here. I don't remember seeing that hole at the bottom left of the stone, do you?" He pointed to a tiny hole that looked like a core might have been taken.

Preston examined it with the magnifying loupe himself. "No, that's new. It was a bear to get this stone polished. I should know, I did it myself. There were no holes, I'm sure. Someone must've taken a sample of my stone for analysis. There's a tool called a micro-core sampler at school. It's used for macro and micro evaluations of dense mineral substances, usually done under a microscope. A sophisticated piece of equipment. That's what that hole looks like to me."

Rachael interjected, "Why would anyone want to do that and how could they do it without your knowledge?"

"It's usually used for elemental analysis. They take the core then use a spectrophotometer to find out what the core is made of. It doesn't take much. Looks like the core sample went through the silver metallic matrix of the stone, not the turquoise. I guess someone wanted to know what that metal was. We always take off all jewelry before we work with machines. Someone could have easily taken it from my locker during class, we never lock anything."

Rachael was hanging on every word, looking fascinated. "You really know about this stuff, Preston. You've become a geologist."

Preston shrugged. "Well, I'm learning."

The President was still trying to piece the puzzle together. "What kind of elements and rare earth stuff might they be looking for?"

"Usually it would be silver associated with turquoise, but it could also be something rare like molybdenum, which is found in New Mexico."

"You're sure Max was working on rare earth elements?"

"Yes," Preston nodded. "Molybdenum would fall into that category, or even rarer elements, anything very uncommon in nature. This stuff could have important uses in technology, things like catalytic convertors, for example. Could be very valuable."

"One more question. Is Max a big-shouldered guy? Short blonde hair, six-feet-plus, nice dresser?" the President asked.

"Yes, that's exactly what he looks like."

The President decided to come clean. "Max is the guy. I have one other thing to share. I didn't want to worry you two, but Max grabbed Roscoe today and not in a nice way. Shoved Roscoe into his van and drove off. I watched it. I was going to follow him, but then Bloom showed up and I followed him instead. I had to know who shot me and I figured Bloom would lead me to you and I had to talk to you. I feel bad I didn't follow Roscoe, but maybe it's not too late."

Rachael narrowed her eyes, absorbing the information.

Preston shook his head in regret. "I'm sorry, Mr. President, I may have been the guy who got you shot."

"Don't sweat it, kid. We just figured out who's after me, which is a good thing. I still don't know why, but I have a stinking suspicion it isn't for turquoise. This is something else. You up for a quick trip to Socorro? I could use your help."

"Whatever I can do. What do you need?"

"I need you to get into the CXI building and see if you can find out what this Max character is working on, anything that points to where he might be or what he's really up to. You think you can do that?"

"Yeah. It's still President's Day weekend and the campus will be a ghost town. I know how to get into that building. I'm the Indian kid, but I'm well liked."

Rachael, who had been listing attentively, stood up. "Listen, both of you, we need to call the police. Roscoe is in serious trouble and I'm worried about Charles. He's not telling me everything. There's something fishy about his backer and this whole fake jewelry thing. He runs to Santa Fe yesterday, then today he goes to meet some partner without saying goodbye. That's not like my Bloom. There's a problem and I'm afraid my husband may be in the thick of it. And now you want Preston spying for you? I don't think so. We need the police involved."

"Rachael," the President said in his most calm voice, "call the police if you have to, but I could use a little time to put this together. Could you just wait a few hours? Think about it. Someone tried to kill me and it's probably Max. He's trying to track me down. He knows Preston is involved, so he's already in danger. Maybe you want to talk with your husband and see if you can find out his story and how it ties in. See what he's hiding. But I need Preston's help, and I need to see if I can find out where Blue and the man who grabbed Roscoe went. Quite frankly, I have a better chance of finding out what's going on than the police right now, who will need to be convinced there's really a problem and who knows how they'll handle it."

"I don't know," Rachael responded dubiously. "I'd like to talk with Bloom, which should be soon I hope. Then we'll decide about calling the cops."

"Yes," the President agreed, "wait and talk to Bloom first."

"I don't like Preston rushing off to Socorro, though. He'll be at more risk there," Rachael objected.

Preston insisted, "It's my decision. I'm helping. I'm going to get into that building and out before anyone gets back to campus." He jumped up from the table and headed for his room.

The President could see he was making progress. The kid was going to help and Rachael was hedging. "I will take the big risks," he assured. "I just need some more information from Preston, and they already know he's involved. Best that he gets there and out during the holiday weekend."

Rachael stared at the President. "I don't like this. Not one bit."

"Nor do I, but we're already in too deep to ignore it."

With a sigh, Rachael rose and walked down the hallway to Preston's room, where he could be heard hastily gathering his belongings. "You're too big and too old to stop, but I don't like this. Promise me you won't take unnecessary risks. And call me once you're down there. If you're taking old Route 6, remember that road can have black ice so don't speed," she told him.

"No problem," Preston responded.

She came back into the living room and began straightening up. "I'll find out what my *bilagaana* husband's keeping from me and fill you in, President. My guess is he thinks he's protecting me, but it's more like he's the one that needs protecting." She smiled.

The President couldn't have managed things better, he thought. "OK, let's get this show on the road. Preston will do his part, and I'll take care of the heavy lifting. Don't you worry."

Preston and the President rushed off to their cars, heading in different directions looking for answers. Meanwhile, Rachael tried to get ahold of Bloom. No response. Just voicemail. She left an urgent message.

CHAPTER 44

AIRPLANE MODE

All alone now and with Bloom unreachable, Rachael's anxiety level escalated tenfold. The rez was notorious for not having very good cell coverage, but still it was not like him to just disappear without checking in. He was either avoiding her, in a bad service area, or worse, in trouble.

Rachael loaded her two kids into the truck and took them over to the trading post for the second time in two days without asking, and implored Sal to watch them. "And if Bloom calls, tell him to phone me immediately. Immediately!" she told Sal. She knew he could tell that she was worried but he didn't press her for details. "Thank you! Thank you so much," she said, before he could ask what was really up.

She hurried back home, boiled water for a strong batch of cowboy coffee, and stared at the stove's antiquated clock. Time suddenly had become important to a woman who had never worn a watch. It would take Preston about three hours to reach Socorro. As soon as Bloom touched base with her, she would call the police. She had promised to wait, but her internal clock was screaming *call now*.

It had been 45 grueling minutes and her second cup of coffee was nearly finished when Rachael heard the front door open. She turned, running to embrace her husband, when she realized the muscular white man shouldering his way through the front door was not Bloom. Shit, was this Max? He was heading for her fast.

Rachael knew she was in trouble. She raced into the kitchen, grabbed the hot coffee off the stove, and flung it in the man's direction. Some of the spray splashed onto the left side of his body. He let out a yell, then smiled sadistically.

"Oh, you're a feisty one, you are. I'm afraid Max is going to make you pay for that," he taunted, approaching closer.

The President hadn't exaggerated. This guy meant to harm her.

Rachael eyeballed her options. She knew the terrain but he was bigger and stronger. There was nowhere to go except to hide behind her weaving loom. She scooted behind it and grabbed the batten she'd stuck between the warps, readying for a last stand.

Max pushed the loom at his intended victim with such force that it toppled over, hitting her hard in the head and pinning Rachael against the wall.

The last thing she remembered was a knife slashing wildly at her tapestry's warps, pinging as the tight wool threads were freed from the pressure of the loom, her only defense from the man who in South Africa was known as Max the Knife.

CHAPTER 45

NOBODY HOME

To Bloom's eye, Roscoe's place upon his second visit of the day looked just as it had when he had left it that morning. But Simplton was trained to notice things he didn't.

Before entering the house, she did a cursory evaluation of the property. "See this," she said, pointing to the ground. "Someone fell here, and hard. See how there is push in the sand? Looks like the person tumbled. You can see two such marks."

She approached the trailer, examining the stairs and determining the trajectory. "The person most likely hit one of these stairs, the first one, bounced and came resting here." She got on her hands and knees. "See here! That's a hand print from the person who was thrown or fell from the trailer. Only one print, not two, very distinctive." She was looking from an angle trying to understand where the other print had gone.

Bloom tried to understand. "So somebody threw Roscoe out of his own home?"

"He was thrown, he must have hurt his arm, one hand was used to get up. See here, it's a drag mark. See these shoe prints? A loafer maybe. The loafer guy pulled him and then it stops. You can see the pressure from the shoe. It was heavy what he was dragging, probably Roscoe. It stops so he put the person into something. From the tire marks, probably a vehicle. This is a crime scene most assuredly. I need to call in forensics before we go any further. I want you to retrace your tracks exactly back to your truck and wait. I can't have any additional footprints screwing up my crime scene. Are the shoes you have on the same ones you were wearing when you were here earlier?"

"Yes, I went home but didn't change shoes." At least he'd done something right. It was at that point, having said the word "home," that Bloom was reminded of Rachael. He needed to call his wife. She would be plenty upset that he had been gone so long and had departed so abruptly.

Back in his truck, he pulled out his phone and realized that it was still in airplane mode. He slid the indicator back on and watched as five messages from Rachael flooded in.

He listened to each message. Each sounded more concerned than the last. The first four messages had come almost exactly 20 minutes apart. The last one was over an hour ago.

"Bloom, you need to call me immediately when you get this," Rachael begged on the last one. "Where are you?" Her voice sounded very worried. "Something's wrong. I'm going to call the police soon if I don't hear from you. Preston's gone to Socorro to find information on Max, and the President has gone to look for Blue and Max. Call me, please. I love you!"

Bloom froze. He dialed Rachael, but the line went to voicemail. "Max," he muttered to himself. The same name written on the paper he'd found under Roscoe's bed. Who was this President? Why was Preston going to Socorro in search of information? How could he have been so stupid as to not turn his phone back on after Simplton's earlier admonishment?

Yelling for Simplton to come quickly, he held his phone out. "Here, listen to my wife's messages."

As she listened, Simplton frowned. Bloom knew it couldn't be good.

CHAPTER 46

IT'S PERSONAL

Pack realized after backtracking to his truck that there wasn't anything he could do in the current situation to help PC. He considered calling the cops, but Pack was not a fan of law enforcement. Instead he would go back to Farmington and see if he could locate the President. He might not be Pack's favorite stone man, but the President had been a decorated Marine in Vietnam and it was his girlfriend in jeopardy. The President would want to handle it in his own way.

The best motel in Farmington was the Holiday Inn Express. Pack was pretty sure this was where the President would be staying. It made sense that PC would have walked from there to get groceries, and she seemed to be heading back in that direction when she was lured into the vehicle.

Pack could be charming when he needed to and today was that time. The front desk had one Indian girl who looked to be about 20, probably Hopi, but she could have been from one of the Rio Grande pueblos.

"Hello, Miss. What a lovely turquoise bracelet. I'm looking for my best friend. He told me to meet him at his room but I left the room number at my house, where I also left my cell phone. Could you try him? It could also be under his girlfriend's name."

Pack was right. They were there. He watched from the side of his eye as the girl punched in the number 235.

"Sorry, no answer. You want to leave a message?"

"I'll come back later, thanks."

Pack found the room at the back of the hotel. He knocked. Silence. Checking outside the nearest door, there were no signs of either PC's vehicle or the President's. Returning to the room, he used his locksmith tools which he always kept in a side pocket of his pack along with his revolver. Pack easily entered room 235.

It was the President's room, no doubt. There was a pale blue travel bag with a tag confirming, "Patsy Clever, Gallup, NM," and men's clothing that had to be the President's.

Pack decided since he was already breaking and entering, he might as well toss the place for anything of interest. He found it in a boot under a heap of clothes: a large quantity of the same non-Indian bracelets that Blue and Bloom had shown him, as well as two nice older Navajo bracelets, one with a blue gem stone, the other some Cerrillos turquoise. No loose turquoise cabs.

The hotel room was clearly the President's current base camp. He would be back. With no number to get ahold of the President, Pack would just have to wait and hope it was soon. He began putting things back in order in the room. No sense aggravating the President and PC.

❋ ❋ ❋ ❋

The President left Rachael's house and decided he would see if he could track down the van that had grabbed Roscoe or if he could find Blue. Both the van and Blue, in his crappy green car, had headed north from Roscoe's trailer. It was a long shot to find either, but the President needed to make progress on some front, and daylight would soon be fading. Once the cops got involved, his #35 turquoise mine would be toast, if it wasn't already.

He hoped that Preston might find some clues as to where the man called Max might be holding Roscoe. There were lots of mining operations in the Southwest, both on and off the Navajo Nation. The closest industrial complex was just south of Farmington at Four Corners Power Plant. There were a couple of mining operations in that area. If Max were a geologist, he might go to one, but which?

The President decided to check in with PC and let her know he would not be back until later and not to worry. He wouldn't share the fact that he thought he was getting closer to finding out who shot him. There was no answer on her cell phone. He tried again. This was unusual, as PC was good about answering and he knew she was worried about him. Then he tried their hotel room. A man answered.

"Is this room 235?"

"Yes, it's me, Pack."

"What the fuck are you doing in my goddamn room, Pack, and where is PC?"

"Where are you, President?"

"I'm headed your fucking way, and not a moment too soon. Where is PC? I'm asking you again."

"Uh, I saw her get what I think was abducted—"

The President interrupted, "What you mean, abducted?"

"Listen, where are you? Are you close to the hotel? It's better if I explain in person. That's why I came here. PC's in trouble and I didn't know what to do so I tracked you down. I'm the good guy here. I'm trying to help."

"You better be, or there will be consequences you won't like. I'll be there in 30 minutes. Stay put and don't do anything stupid. No cops, at least not yet."

Pack understood that it had become personal, which meant that the cops would indeed better be left out of it.

CHAPTER 47

NICE PHOTOGRAPH

Preston made very good time to Socorro. He did encounter black ice, but Rachael's warning made him wary so he didn't lose control. He called Rachael's phone. No answer. As promised, he left a message letting her know he had arrived safely. His adrenaline was pumping.

He had been in the CXI industrial building on a couple of occasions with Professor Heard, the department head who had access to all the buildings. Preston had seen Heard retrieve his keys from his front desk drawer. A big ball of keys opened all the buildings, including the off-limits CXI complex.

Hopefully the keys would be left there over the holiday weekend. It was only mid-afternoon on Sunday and no one was around campus. Preston felt he owed it to the President to find out something, seeing as he'd set all this trouble in motion with his own big mouth.

Well, no way to get in but to break a glass pane so he could open the door from the inside. He put on his glove and did the deed using the back of his hand to break the small pane. OK, no alarm. Good. Preston hurried to the inner sanctum of the man who might be expelling him in the coming days.

In the drawer, just as he remembered, were the keys. Finding the correct one was easy as it had "CXI" written on it in black marker.

Preston hurried over to the CXI building, still not sighting a single soul on campus. Inside, the building's only light was cast via high glass windows that made it feel like an ancient chapel. The building itself was industrial but in a modern way. It was an expensive, unique building, designed by some well-known architect, and not to Preston's taste.

There were numerous offices and cubicles, all surrounding an expansive laboratory in the center of the building. Small brass tags on each door posted the occupant's name. None were for Solenhosen. After circling them all, Preston went into one. What was this person responsible for, and how close were they to Max? He rifled around, finding folders of phone bills, electric bills, tax information, and memos about budgets. It became apparent searching each of these offices would be a waste of time. It would be light for only another couple of hours, and once it got dark Preston couldn't risk turning on the lights. Security, no matter how flimsy, might see him.

As Preston circled the premises again, he noticed an office off to the side by itself. No name was on the door, which was more substantial than the rest: a heavy, metal door that was locked. Preston methodically went through Dr. Heard's key ring till he found one marked X. It slid in, opening the door to a spacious office.

Inside, large animal heads from all parts of Africa were mounted on the walls. There were numerous photos of Max, always standing next to another tall, distinguished man or group of men, and some with soccer players. In one of the images was Dr. Heard. This one appeared to be taken in some expensive restaurant. It showed Max, Dr. Heard, and an older distinguished-looking CEO type, all smiling.

A massive file cabinet beckoned to Preston. There was a single file drawer, which was locked. None of Dr. Heard's keys worked, so Preston took out a tool he worked on jewelry with that was attached to his pocketknife. He managed to pick the lock open.

Now that he was inside the drawer, he found numerous files, all with official-looking seals, as well as some maps. One map showed the area that looked to be near Crownpoint. It was a detailed mineral map, with elevations and copious notes. This was the same general location at which Preston had found the stone on Hastiin Begay's land. Relief flooded through him.

Preston scooped up all the files and stuffed them in a modern-looking trashcan. Using newspapers from South Africa that were already in the can, he covered up the files he was stealing.

Before he left, he snatched the picture of Heard off the wall and slipped it into his jacket packet. The photo was evidence of some kind, none of which was probably admissible in court now that he had stolen it, but maybe it would help the President or himself when the shit hit the fan.

Preston dashed out of the building and ran to his car, breathing heavily. Still panting, he headed north, back to Toadlena. He figured his geology career, not to mention his freedom, was probably very much in peril. Distinguishing between right and wrong had never been so difficult for the college sophomore.

CHAPTER 48

BLOODY LOOM

Bloom watched as Simplton listened to Rachael's messages for a second time. The concern in Rachael's voice and the time that had elapsed since her last call said it all. Something was very wrong.

Since he couldn't reach Rachael, Bloom called Preston. As Simplton listened in on speakerphone, they got an abbreviated recap about the turquoise, the President's visit, and Max Solenhosen. Preston reported that he had just removed Max's files and was heading home. He would be there just after sundown. He had not heard from Rachael since he'd left.

Simplton ordered Preston not to further touch any of the files he had stolen. They were evidence in a kidnapping case with which he was now intimately involved. He was ordered to go directly to Rachael and Bloom's home and nowhere else. There would be an FBI officer waiting there to take possession of the files. He was not to share anything with anyone.

"Now my whole family's dragged into this, goddamnit," Bloom exploded at Simplton.

She calmly called to divert two FBI officers to Bloom's house.

"And we want the tribal police over there, too," Bloom requested.

Then she ordered Bloom to get into her car, leaving his truck in front of Roscoe's. She would drive them back to his home.

Bloom hated to be stuck with this woman, especially in a car that had no four-wheel drive and obviously was a Fed vehicle, but she was in charge and he needed her help.

Once sequestered in her car and in between listening to her various conversations, it didn't take long for Bloom to pump her for more details. Firstly, Max Solenhosen was an ex-special forces officer from South Africa, with a background in mining engineering. He worked for the CEO of the CXI corporation. Max's title identified him as head of security operations. His file was spotty, but from what Shirley had seen, he was not a man to mess with. His nickname was Max the Knife.

Simplton put out an APB out for Max, listing him as armed and extremely dangerous. She also put an APB out for the President. She was not aware of any issues with the President. He had a distinguished military record, including a purple heart, but was a man who could be in serious trouble. With his background, he might be looking to even a score.

Bloom called the Toadlena Post to see if Sal knew anything about Rachael's whereabouts. Sal said he had been watching the kids for nearly two hours and had not heard anything from Rachael. She had said she was waiting to hear from Bloom and she seemed very worried.

Trying not to sound alarmist, Bloom explained, "Rachael might be delayed, Sal. Could you watch the kids for a bit longer? I'm in the middle of something important that I can't discuss." He hoped Sal could tell from his voice that it was serious.

"Got it," Sal agreed. "I can keep them at my house for the night. I've got milk from the last time Rachael brought them over. No worries. You know Willy thinks of the post as his second home, and the wife loves having a baby around."

Bloom was relieved that his young children were safe and thanked Sal profusely. That taken care of, he turned to Shirley. "Something terrible has happened to Rachael. I just know it."

Bloom and Simplton arrived at Bloom's home to find the two FBI agents already on the scene, accompanied by the local tribal police. It wasn't a pretty picture. Orange cones with police investigation tape had been set up next to the Yellowhorse-Bloom welcoming tire. A couple of neighbors were already gathered to watch.

The authorities had found the stove burner on, the coffee pot broken on the ground, coffee everywhere, the broken loom, and a ripped Navajo weaving tossed to the floor. They were in the process of gathering evidence.

Seeing the devastation to Rachael's weaving, Bloom teared up. It was a masterpiece that had been ruined. Worse yet, it was clear that there had been some sort of struggle. For Rachael to let her rug be destroyed was an ominous sign. There was a trace of blood on the loom, which solidified in Bloom's mind that his wife was in serious trouble or even dead. He tried to explain the significance and how Rachael would have defended her weaving, but Simplton was busy gathering intelligence from the cops. He fingered the ripped weaving, tears welling up in his eyes.

"OK, Bloom," Shirley finally pulled him outside the home where they could talk privately. "Here's what we know so far. A blue van was spotted here by one of your neighbors. It arrived not long after Rachael returned from Sal's, maybe 2:30. There is no sign of any bodily fluids other than a small amount on the wooden loom, but obviously there was a struggle. We think she was probably abducted, possibly the same scenario as with Roscoe. The detective on the scene at Roscoe's place has confirmed what I had thought. They did find traces of blood on the ground there, and on one of the steps, which we are analyzing. It's a very small amount. Roscoe's gun and money were just where you said they were. It's likely both Roscoe and Rachael were kidnapped by the same person, probably not harmed in the process, just overpowered."

Bloom was so angry he was shaking. "You know Simplton, I hold you responsible. You brought me into this fiasco and I expect you to get my wife out of it, alive and unharmed."

"I know, I'm terribly sorry, I can't tell you how badly I feel," she replied, showing Bloom a side he finally liked.

She grabbed his arm. "I will do everything I can to help you and your family. As soon as Preston gets here, I want you to take him somewhere safe where you can have some quiet time with him. Usually these things play out in fairly quick succession. Max has Rachael, would be my guess. At this point, he probably doesn't know we are looking for her, which is in your wife's favor. I will stay in close touch with you and protect you. I need to know if anyone contacts you. Why don't you think about where you're going to take Preston when he gets here." She squeezed his arm reassuringly.

Bloom nodded in agreement, glad to have something constructive on which to focus.

CHAPTER 49

NO-WIN SITUATION

Max Solenhosen was trying to figure out his next move as well, an unusual predicament for a man who was always was one step ahead of the competition. He'd strangled Leroy when that chatterbox proved too disruptive, then dumped his body in the incinerator at the power plant.

Then he'd picked up Roscoe this morning, and when he'd started with that distracting chanting, Max had broken his neck, nice and quiet, then dragged him out to that same incinerator. Roscoe knew too much. There was no rehabilitating him. Folks would probably figure the old alkie had gotten into trouble he couldn't get out of. It was unlikely many people would mourn the foul-smelling fellow.

PC was a different story. He'd picked up the pretty dishwater blonde as bait, pure and simple. He was hoping to use her to lure in the President, so he could stop his meddling. She was currently tied up and tranquilized at the power plant.

As he lugged Rachael's inert body into the same hiding spot, Max grunted. He enjoyed the physical labor as well as thriving on the mental logistics.

Rachael was still barely responsive due to his expert handiwork. After banging her head into the loom, he had hit her at close range with the Taser directly in the chest, and luckily she was still conked out, which made her easier to carry upstairs.

The burns on his left arm were probably 1st and 2nd degree, painful but not serious enough to require any medical care other than a clean tee-shirt bandage. Luckily Max had been wearing his coat, which had deflected the sting of the hot coffee.

He had hoped to find Preston at the Bloom-Yellowhorse residence. The kid was a loose end that needed to be tied up. If he wasn't there, then the mother, Rachael, was the next best thing. She would be able to give him the information he needed to determine how much was known and where to find Preston, then he would dispose of all human evidence necessary.

Max understood it wouldn't take long before the cops would get wind of his activities. One mysterious Gallup disappearance then three subsequent abductions in northwestern New Mexico in a single day couldn't stay undetected very long.

The Yellowhorse woman in particular would be missed. There had been toys everywhere at her house, but no kids. Someone must be watching them, and probably only for a few hours. He was glad he hadn't had to deal with kids. Too many bodies, too many distractions. Even if he found out where Preston was, now it was probably too dangerous to make a second visit.

Reff had been notified of a potential problem. The boss was not happy. A 'copter had been put on alert and would be sent in if need be to evacuate Max, who had diplomatic immunity. It wasn't as if Max was in any real danger of being jailed for any significant time, especially if no evidence was found.

As soon as the Yellowhorse woman came around, Max would extract whatever information she had, just like he had done with Roscoe, and probably dispose of her body likewise in the incinerator. For now, he tied her up tight with duct tape just like he had PC, including over their mouths.

PC would likely face the same fate at Rachael, as would her aging boyfriend, the President. Yes, the President had to be dealt with. He could not be allowed to live, knowing the source of the molybdenum and iridium, even if he didn't realize it yet. He would figure it out, he was persistent and smart.

Max laughed at how small-minded these stone men were. The iridium underneath the surface turquoise was the real find. One gram of iridium was worth a thousand times the value of #35.

The operation just outside of the reservation was currently processing a million dollars a day in just iridium, one of the rarest earth minerals on the planet and a crucial component in high-tech gadgets. The molybdenum vein was huge and could add an additional five hundred thousand dollars a day. If the CXI industrial corporation could get access to the rest of the deposit that ran on the reservation, it would easily be one of the richest mines in the world of its type. As far as CXI was concerned, the turquoise was nothing more than slag.

Turning out fake Indian jewelry to try to destroy the local Navajo economy and thus make the locals more likely to assign mineral rights to a very generous benefactor that was willing to support the local chapter houses seemed like a poorly conceived plan in retrospect. It had worked in other countries, destroying the micro economy then bringing in big money to bail the inhabitants out and make them dependent. It was not much different than what the military had done to America's Native cultures in the 1870s.

The fake jewelry they had made was excellent, but it wasn't up to par with the Navajos'. Roscoe had told Max that not only did the man he now knew to be the President understand they were fake, so had the Yellowhorse woman, who wasn't even a silversmith. Max was angry that the powers-to-be hadn't heeded his insider's warnings.

He had cautioned CXI that there were too many variables. It was too hard to destroy a culture of silversmiths with a 130-year-old tradition of making jewelry. If only they had listened, he wouldn't be stuck in this no-win position now. Just bribe the local government with huge money, instead of such a hare-brained scheme. However, his job was cleanup and cleanup he would do.

As Rachael started to come to, Max got out his whetting stone. He had some more carving to take care of.

CHAPTER 50

A PROMISE IS MADE

Pack could hear the President's truck speed into the parking lot. The tires squealed as the President applied the brakes. Pack had decided to take his gun out of his hidden museum flap and lay it on the table far away as he didn't want any misunderstandings. He truly was the good guy in this situation, even if he may have been on the President's trail to get one of his precious #35 stones.

The door flew open and the President's eyes scanned wildly around the room. He had a Glock cocked in his right hand, and a 10-inch buck knife in his left. Pack was sitting motionless on the bed. He was glad the gun was not in his hand. It could have prompted a very bad outcome.

"OK, give it to me. What the fuck's going on?" the President demanded.

Pack explained every detail of what he had seen and why he was sitting on the bed and his gun was on the table far away.

The President soaked it in, absorbing the details. "How many cars did you see at the plant? How many buildings?"

"Just a dark blue van. Two buildings, one bigger, maybe 2,000 square feet. And a small 600-foot storage shed sort of structure."

"Only one window, is that correct?"

"Yes I saw only one, but it was big enough to see the man that grabbed PC holding a knife. I think the guy I saw is the same one that came up to me at the Gem and Mineral Show, a guy named Max. He was looking for you and told me he would pay me a hundred bucks for information. I can't be positive, but it seemed like he had the same features. I have a card with his info. The card was like something you print at Kinko's." Pack extended the card. In black letters it said: *CXI, Max Solenhosen, 505.820.7451.* Underneath it, scrawled in blue ink: *$100, info on the President.*

"Shit, this is the same asshole that the Yellowhorse kid told me about. OK, now I got a serious question to ask you, Pack, and I want a fucking straight answer. Why were you looking for PC and what's in it for you?" The President stared at him, looking for the answer before Pack opened his mouth.

Pack understood the gravity of the question and kept his eyes locked with the President's. "I wanted one of those #35 stones. I tried to buy Leroy's. He wouldn't sell it. I have to have one for my museum. That's it. I didn't expect to see PC get nabbed, but I wasn't going to let her go down without me doing something to help. That's everything."

The President didn't say a word. Then he reached in the pouch around his neck and opened it up, bringing out a #35 cab. He tossed it over to Pack. "You help me get PC back alive and this is yours."

Pack's eyes never left the stone, a huge grin spreading on his face despite the severity of the situation. Pack examined the stone, his eyes glued on the gem.

The President grabbed the gem back. "When we get PC back alive."

Pack assured, "I'm here to help, stone or no stone. I would give my right arm for that cab, but I'd rather get PC back in one piece. She's my friend, too."

"Pack, ol' buddy, I hope you don't have to. Now let's get going. PC is in serious danger."

Soon they would find out she wasn't the only one.

❄ ❄ ❄ ❄

The President and Pack climbed into the President's truck and headed west out of Farmington on U.S. Highway 64 toward the power plant and the Navajo Reservation.

Halfway there, Preston called to give the President the scoop on the files he'd stolen and what Bloom had told him was going down at home with the FBI.

"Preston, I know you're risking a lot calling me but I need your help, and it sounds like Rachael does, too," the President advised, taking charge of a hellish situation that kept worsening.

"You're going have to trust me, but the FBI is not your friend. They worry about their asses, not ours. I, on the other hand, am worried about *us*. I have skin in this game. The woman I love has been abducted. I've got the firepower, the training, and the balls to take down that bastard Max. What I need is what you have, those records. I guarantee somewhere in those files there is something that ties this Max guy to some pretty big people. It looks like the department head of your school is involved and god knows who else. You can't turn those over to the FBI. We need them as leverage to get your mom and my girlfriend and Roscoe out of this madman's hands. Will you help?"

"You mean, don't go home?"

"Exactly. I understand this is one of those life choices that no matter what you decide, will have serious consequences. You've got to go with your gut. But I promise you, Rachael's safety is paramount to me. She's probably with PC right now and I'm headed there to get both of them out safely."

"OK," Preston gulped. "Where do you want to meet? I'll bring the files. I have to help Rachael, no matter what. You have to promise me, President, that you will find her and help her, just like your girlfriend. Will you do that, give me your word?"

"Yes, I will give you my word, even if it costs me dearly. I will save your mom and PC and even Roscoe, but he's last on the list, as he really is beyond saving, if you ask me."

"Fair enough, but Roscoe helped me when I was a kid so I have to have his back, too."

"I'll do my best," the President promised. "You know the APS Four Corners Power Plant west of Farmington? You want to meet at the water tank?"

"I know it," Preston concurred. "It's tagged in pink letters by one of the local gangs. I'll floor it and get there in less than an hour. I need to let Bloom know what's going on, though."

"Yes, a man has a right to know what's happening to his wife. Tell him we're going to try and handle it ourselves but if we don't work out a deal then he should bring the cops. I would think an hour should be enough time. He doesn't know me, but let him know I made a promise to you and I expect to keep it."

CHAPTER 51

THESE ARE MY TERMS

Bloom was still pacing at the house as dusk darkened the premises. Then Preston called.

"Why aren't you here yet?" Bloom demanded.

"Um, on my way to Farmington," Preston explained, offering a rundown of what was happening.

It was a plan Bloom didn't like. An end run around the FBI by an 18-year-old? Bloom was not a fan of Simplton's, but she did seem competent at her job. Now Preston was putting himself at risk for a man Bloom knew nothing about. Plus there was no proof that Rachael was there, although it was likely. Bloom respected Preston's resolve but hoped if Rachael was there, he wouldn't be putting her at further risk.

"I know where those buildings are," Bloom said. "There are some great petroglyphs on the other side of the mesa. It's an hour's drive from here. The sun will be down by then. I'm going to give you guys a 20-minute lead, then I'm going to take Simplton there. Just her. She's not going to like it and I'm probably going to get myself in hot water, just like you are."

"I just want this over with," said Preston.

Bloom tried to make light of the situation. "Maybe we can bunk together at the pen."

Then he added, "Seriously, try to negotiate a deal, if possible. Keep your head low and please keep out of the line of fire. I understand it's your aunt and I trust you. If you have any good luck fetishes, keep them close. Text me if you can."

Bloom surprised himself that he would think in terms of fetishes for protection at time like this. But he still had the one that Hastiin Sherman had given him years ago and he believed it did have powers he couldn't understand. Today was a day you needed everything in your arsenal to be able to outwit a bad coyote spirit.

※ ※ ※ ※

Twenty minutes felt like an hour. Then Bloom found Simplton and pulled her aside, next to her official car. It was a conversation that he was not looking forward to.

"OK, Charlie, what do you need. You know we're trying to gather valuable information here, and time is precious. Have you heard from Preston? He should have been here by my now."

"Yes, I have heard from Preston. He's not coming. This is what I want to discuss with you."

"What do you mean, not coming? This is not a game. Your nephew is in serious legal trouble."

"I fully understand that, as does Preston, but this is not about doing what he is told. This is about making a decision to save his aunt and my wife, and while I don't agree with it, I am standing by him. So this is what I have to say, and you're not going to like it but my terms are nonnegotiable—jail time, list, whatever, we're talking my terms."

"Your terms? You have no idea what you're doing! You can say good bye to your little Canyon Road gallery, for starters," Simplton exploded.

"Look, I know where Max, probably Rachael, Roscoe, and someone named PC are hiding. The President is en route there and going to try and make a deal, trading files for hostages. If they can't make it happen peaceably, then he'll probably resort to force. It's all going down any minute now. I will take you and only you to the place. Otherwise the deal is off."

"Bloom, we need backup," Simplton protested.

"If you want to do the deal, let's get in the car right now and go to my truck, then we will go to the place. That's the deal. Otherwise, cuff me."

Simpleton's eyes squinted hard as she stared at Bloom, sizing up the situation. "OK, let's go. I hope you know what you're doing, because your ass is way out there, as well as mine. If it goes badly, you'll do hard time, you can be sure of that."

"If it goes badly, Shirley, hard time will be the least of my concerns."

CHAPTER 52

LET'S MAKE A DEAL

Preston arrived with the trashcan of files and hopped in the President's truck. The President moved over so Pack could drive now, as he knew the way. Meanwhile, the President rummaged through the files. These were his trade bait.

There were numerous classified documents from the CXI industrial corporation to companies in a variety of countries, including China, Syria, Australia, and many American corporations. One file talked of "Indian style jewelry to help encourage local Native inhabitants to grant mineral rights." Stapled to that file was a detailed map of Hastiin Begay's land, pinpointing deposits. The file also had names of numerous other Navajos. Each name had one or more stars next to it, from one to five. There was one star next to Begay, which the President figured meant he was least likely to cooperate.

With Preston's help, the President was able to decipher the maps showing probable veins of iridium, as well as CXI's current mine. It was a treasure trove of information, exactly the proverbial smoking gun the President had hoped for.

It was enough that Max would have to listen. The President took photos with his smart phone, and then emailed the copies to his computer as insurance. The President had embraced technology, unlike his fellow stone men. It might mean the difference in his pulling off the trade tonight.

When Pack got within a quarter mile of the location, he turned off the lights and slowed down the truck to a crawl. There was nearly a full moon, which would work to their favor, they hoped.

"OK, listen up," the President whispered. "The plan is that I will call Max to try and use the files as a bargaining chip to release the hostages. Here, Preston, take my buck knife. If we're able to pull off the trade, your job is to bring the truck up as the getaway vehicle. The backup plan is for Pack and I to rush the house. In that case, I'll go through the front door and Pack will break the window and start shooting. Preston, you are to stay in the truck. If we rush the place, then drive hard at the house with the truck, ramming it if necessary, to pick up whomever comes out. If no one comes out, it means that we've failed. Head to the Farmington police department and call Bloom."

The President knew it was a dicey plan at best, but it was all he could come up with. He was running out of time and ideas.

The two stone men left the truck quietly, picking their way on foot closer to the building, following the same route Pack had taken earlier. They split up once they got to the dirt driveway. The President took off his sling, stretched his right arm a couple of times, then wrapped the sling around his head. He was sixtysomething but he was as ready for battle as he'd ever been. Pack clutched most of the files, except for the crucial smoking-gun file. This one was tucked into the back of the President's pants.

The large building had one window illuminated. No one was visible, but human sounds were audible.

Using the New Mexico phone number that Max had given Pack back during the gem show, the President picked out the digits. He prayed for enough coverage to complete the call. He was glad he had recently switched to Verizon for better coverage. It might be the difference between life and death. What an advertisement it would make: "When your life depends on it, can you hear me now?"

The President and Pack listened as the phone rang faintly in the distance. Out there in the darkness, they could just barely discern the duck-quack ring tone. Max was here.

CHAPTER 53

BAD MOON RISING

The sun was down and the moon was rising toward Table Mesa as Bloom and Simplton raced north on U.S. Route 491. It would have made for a wonderful photograph if weren't for the horrific circumstances.

Bloom kept emphasizing Simplton was not to use her phone for backup: she had gotten them into this mess and only she would get them out. He didn't want helicopters swooping down and getting his wife killed. Bloom respected the law but he also knew sometimes there were better ways to handle things on the Navajo Reservation.

He found the small dirt road he knew was just south of the tiny Shiprock Airport runway. They headed east towards Farmington. It would save them 10 minutes if he didn't hit a cow grazing on the open pasture. It was a risk, but the night was going to be full of risks. Hopefully this would not be the one that would take them down.

For the first time since getting in his truck, Simplton said something. "You really love her, don't you?"

"Yes, with all my heart. If it wasn't for Rachael, I would never have found my *hozho*."

"You know, I envy you, even though you may go to prison for this hare-brained scheme. I envy what you have, an unfettered love for someone. It's hard being in law enforcement and living for the job, to find something like that. I'm never in one place long enough to find someone to have a long-lasting relationship with. I wish I had a family like you."

Bloom was surprised at Simplton's frankness. He wondered if she might realize at that moment that life was short and tonight might be Bloom's last one with his wife, or for that matter, both of theirs. It was a sobering moment.

"Shirley, we are going to save my wife and you will find someone. I believe this with my heart. I can't explain how, but I just feel it."

"I hope you're right, Charlie. I hope you're right."

CHAPTER 54

THE GAMBIT

Max answered his phone. The trepidation was evident in his voice, along with his South African accent. "Hello?"

Relieved, the President and Pack backed away from the building into the trees so they wouldn't be heard or seen. The President assumed quiet control. "Max, you've been looking for me, and you've been a bad boy. It's the President. You and I need to talk."

"Nice to hear from you. This saves me having to find you. I guess since you have this number, you might have a few other surprises for me. I know I do for you."

Perfect. The President decided to lay out his cards and hope he had assessed the situation correctly. "Yes, I know you have three hostages, I know about your bogus jewelry scam, and I know about the iridium. I know about it all."

There was a pause.

"I see, you do surprise me. That doesn't happen very often. So what now?"

The President and Pack watched the window as Max walked by it, a gun in one hand, the cell phone in the other, pacing. The President thought about shooting him, but that could wait. He was in command and didn't know the full gravity of the situation at this point.

"I have all your files. You know, the ones back at the university. I have them all. I want to make a trade. The hostages for the files, and we walk away. No hard feelings. I stay the fuck out of your iridium find forever with my couple of little turquoise stones, and you stop grabbing people off the streets. What do you say?"

"Hum, that's interesting, but how do I know you won't want to go sticking your nose back where it isn't wanted? Iridium can be irresistible. There are powers that you can't imagine behind this. No stone man or Indian is going to get in the way of my job. So how can you assure me you'll go away for good?"

"You have my word. I'll step back, that's all I can do. I can't control anything but me, but that I can do."

"Where are you, Herr President?"

"Do we have a deal, Max?"

"Yes, a deal, where are you?"

"I'm right outside your door. Open up and I'll come in."

"Bravo, you are a brave man. You are free to enter. I'm waiting for you."

"By the way, Max, if you shoot me you will never find all the files." The President knew Max had to be considering doing just that, but would think better of it after the President's warning.

The President walked up to the building, leaving Pack in the darkness. He stepped to the side of the door and turned the handle then pushed the door open with his boot. He waited for a hail of bullets. His injured arm was throbbing but he barely noticed it.

Nothing happened. He wasn't shot at. Max was going to play it square. The President stepped inside.

The tall man with the foreign accent was directly in front of him, an impressive figure. At the far side of the room were Rachael and PC, both tied up, both gagged with duct tape but alert and alive.

The President was within 15 feet of Max, both of them clutching their guns. The President knew that Pack would be watching, and could be the difference.

"OK, so where are my files, the ones you took without asking?" Max commanded.

"First, I say we put the guns down. I'll put mine on the floor in front of me if you do the same. We both come up slowly. That way no one gets trigger happy. Everything is good. We talk, we take care of business, then you get your files."

"OK, Mr. President, we can do it your way."

Both men placed their guns on the linoleum floor, their eyes never breaking contact.

"Now, my files please," Max requested.

"Pack," the President called out. "Please come in with the files."

They waited. Pack's nearing footsteps could be heard, along with the sound of a truck pulling closer. Then Pack came in the door carrying the trash can, his ever-present pack on his shoulder and a gun in his belt.

"No hero shit, just give the man the files. We get the girls and we get out of here," ordered the President.

Pack slid the trash can over to Max, and stood next to the President.

Max took a quick glance at the files and seemed satisfied, meanwhile keeping his eye on the men.

The President repeated, "Let us have the girls and we're good. I take it Roscoe won't be coming with us, seeing as he's nowhere in sight?"

"I'm afraid, Herr President, Roscoe and Leroy are unavailable. You didn't know about my meeting with Leroy, did you? He had a big mouth. In any case, both those gentleman had prior engagements. Pressing engagements, you could say. Since we are laying the cards on the table now, is this going to be a problem?"

"Roscoe was never my concern. Too bad about Leroy, but you're right, he should have kept his mouth shut. I came here for the girls. Only the girls."

"I heard a vehicle. Who is driving? You are making me nervous. Who else is out there?"

"It's Rachael's nephew, Preston. He's driving my truck, that's all. He's not armed, just here to get his aunt."

"Tell him to come in. I want to see all the players."

"Preston," the President yelled. "Come in." The engine shut off. Footsteps approached. "We've made the trade. Walk in slowly," he shouted.

A few minutes later, Preston walked through the door, the President's knife stuffed into his back pocket. He saw Rachael and started to go over to her.

"Stop now, Preston," Max ordered. "We need to go slowly. One step at a time. Mr. Pack, please place your gun down on the floor. Then we will make our trade."

Just as Pack put his gun down, both Rachael's and PC's eyes got larger as they stared at the door. They were trying to say something despite their gags.

The President knew something was going wrong. His gut was telling him so. He turned toward whoever was walking in the door unexpectedly.

He felt the tear of a bullet at the same time as he heard the bang. The pain was intense, hitting his good arm, bone breaking. There would be no flesh wound this time.

The President's instinct for survival took over. He rolled head-first to take cover behind a threadbare couch. His gun was on the floor where he could see it he but couldn't quite reach it.

A second bang occurred. Pack, who had reached for his own gun after watching the President get shot, had turned to shoot the shooter but it was too late.

Max had already grabbed his gun and the bullet hit Pack in the back. Pack crashed to the floor with a thump and never moved again.

In the chaos, Preston darted to Rachael's side, knelt beside her, and took out his knife to cut her hands free. She grabbed the open knife from him in her right hand, keeping her hands behind her back as if still tied, then motioned him back.

Max kicked the President's gun away. "OK, Herr President, it's all over. Stand up if you can. Don't make me come to you and shoot you like a dog."

The President struggled to his feet. He couldn't believe who had shot him, who was Max's secret ally in his scheme and had fired now not to warn, but to do serious damage.

CHAPTER 55

CHANGING IT UP

The tables had dramatically turned. Max was now in charge.

"Preston, get up and step away from the girls. Go stand near the President. Keep your hands up or I will be forced to shoot you and as you can tell by Mr. Pack's dead body, I'm a good shot and will not hesitate to kill you. I'm disappointed in you, Preston. You could have been a great asset for the corporation, a Navajo geologist. I would have loved for you to help us strip the wealth from your people. You would have become rich, a king in a land of poverty. Instead, I will probably have to take your promising life away from you."

Preston stepped back, keeping his hands up as told, clearly knowing he was in serious trouble.

Max nodded at his accomplice, "Nice work, Mr. Blue. Your timing for once was impeccable. Too bad you're not much of an assassin. That's twice that you've missed your mark."

Curling his lips into a slight smile, Max watched as the President swayed, his left arm dangling by his side as a flow of dark blood puddled at his feet.

The President glared at the new arrival. "What the fuck, Blue? Why are you working with this mercenary? You're a stone man, for god's sake, not a killer."

Blue would not make eye contact. He held his gun at his side and deferred to Max.

"I can answer this question, Herr President. Blue here was helping me distribute the spurious jewelry. He was our point man for the entire operation and had turned into a nice double agent as well. If you hadn't been so damn persistent, you would have never gotten shot to begin with. I had promised Mr. Blue he would get all the profits from the jewelry sales, then you had to start looking for that turquoise vein on Begay's property, your so-called #35. You know it's an insignificant find, nothing compared to what's underneath... iridium. So I told old Blue here that I would throw in the turquoise vein minus any iridium as part of the deal. He could even keep some of the molybdenum in the turquoise. It's not silver in your #35 that makes it glitter and hard as nails, it's molybdenum with a touch of iridium. Much more valuable elements than your precious turquoise."

Max knew he was saying more than he needed to, but the idiocy of these stone men exasperated him. "So Mr. Blue here gets his turquoise after we're done getting what we want, but to receive the bonus he had one simple task: to take care of you."

Shaking his head, Max lamented, "He followed you for weeks, an excellent tracker and in very good shape, I might add. He walked in from our adjacent mine every day you showed up, patiently following you. I told him to just dispose of you but he insisted he would wait and see if you discovered the turquoise. I guess he hoped you would just give up. But you didn't and then you found the nugget, and unfortunately his marksmanship was less than promised. He also failed to take care of Mr. Leroy after I gave him explicit orders to do so. The only good information was where to find your woman." Max glanced over at Blue who was looking downward.

When Blue raised his head, it was to meet the President's gaze. "Sorry JFK," Blue muttered. "I hoped you wouldn't find any of the stones, I really did. All I wanted was the fake jewelry profit and a new truck. I hated the thought of killing you. Poor Leroy, well, he couldn't help himself, had to show us the #35 cab you gave him. He was so proud, it's too damn bad. And Pack, hell, he was my friend. He shouldn't have been here. That one's on your conscience. But I am sorry about PC."

"That's touching, Mr. Blue," Max scoffed. "But it's all beside the point. This is business, not personal. To make me go down to Gallup to cover up your loose ends with Leroy was a lack of professionalism."

With that, Max pointed the gun straight at Blue, whose attention he'd successfully obtained, and pulled the trigger, destroying instantaneously one of his blue eyes. Blood and brains splattered on the wall behind him as Blue crumpled onto the once-white linoleum tiles.

Max nodded his head, pleased. "Just like that, aim and shoot. It's not hard, it's the job. Nothing personal."

Now Max eyeballed the President and Preston. "OK, with that unfortunate piece of business out of the way, it's time to find out what you know."

Maintaining his aplomb as if nothing unusual had just happened, Max barked, "Herr President, turn around and face the wall. Keep that right arm where I can see it. Nothing stupid or I will shoot you in the knee. Preston, go stand next to him. Not too close. Turn and face the wall, slowly. We don't need any dead heroes."

The two did as they were told.

"I see, Herr President, you didn't give me all the files, did you? Take that file out of your pants and drop it on the floor," Max instructed, smiling now that he was orchestrating the situation. Time was running out for the hostages. He knew it and they probably suspected it.

CHAPTER 56

BANG, BANG, BANG

Just as Bloom pulled up next to the President's empty truck outside the power plant, he and Simplton witnessed Preston walking into the building's front door.

They jumped out of Bloom's truck and started making their way toward the structure, staying quiet and in the shadows.

As they got closer to the building, they saw Blue exit a small utility shed behind the main building and enter the same door Preston had just walked through. Blue was brandishing a 38-caliber revolver near chest level. Shortly after he entered, two shots rang out. Two minutes later, there was another shot.

"I have to call this in," Simplton whispered. Bloom didn't protest. The situation was deteriorating quickly. Bloom had a sick feeling in his stomach that he had screwed up by not listening to Simplton to begin with. After she radioed in their coordinates, she turned to Bloom.

"Listen, I'm going in."

He nodded, "Me too."

"It would be better if you hide in the truck. I've got to level with you. We've had our suspicions that Blue was bad from the get-go. I'm sorry I couldn't tell you, but that's the way the game is played. The good guys are on their way."

"I'm coming," Bloom insisted.

"Stay behind me," she emphasized.

Bloom grabbed her arm, his hands trembling. He leaned over and kissed her on the forehead and whispered, "Shirley, please save my family."

She seemed surprised he could still be so generous after all she had put him through. "I'll do my best, or die trying."

Bloom believed she meant it.

✳ ✳ ✳ ✳

The front door was ajar. Simplton could see two people against a wall. A muscular man who had to be Max Solenhosen was holding a gun to the largest individual's head. There were two bodies on the floor, presumably Max's work. One was Blue and he was obviously dead, a portion of his brains blown out. A large pool of fresh blood had formed around his head and was making a rivulet near the door. She would have to be careful not to slip on the mess when she made her grand entrance.

There were two women tied up in the corner: hostages. Simplton was trying to get their attention when the Navajo woman, who had to be Rachael Yellowhorse, slowly lifted herself off the ground. Her hand ties had been cut, and she was brandishing a large, open hunting knife.

Rachael crept forward toward Max, who was perusing the file that had been in the President's pants, his eyes checking upward every few seconds. Max's back was to the knife-wielding woman. She was going to make a play at Max the Knife, provoking a trained killer with a knife of her own!

Rachael Yellowhorse lunged, the knife blade aiming for the back of Max's neck. Hearing something, Max turned agilely just in time to avoid the full fury of the blade's impact. Instead of dealing a fatal blow, the sharp steel grazed his side, cutting through clothes and flesh, opening an angry wound along his flank. He shrieked in pain as he jumped away. Ignoring the injury, keeping one eye on the President and the other on Rachael, he yelled, "You die now! No Indian squaw hurts me twice."

He aimed his gun at Rachael's head, but Shirley Simplton hit her mark first.

Two bullets pierced Max's upper chest in rapid succession, knocking him onto the ground. He fell over Pack's body into a kind of grotesque, bloody art piece.

Rachael perched in a cat position, breathing hard, knife at the ready. She was trying desperately to figure out what had just happened and whom she would attack next.

"FBI! No one move!" Simplton yelled as she rose from her own crouched shooting position near the door's entrance, stepping into the room and pulling out her badge to show her audience.

"Everyone is OK. I'm Detective Shirley Simplton of the FBI," she instructed as she walked into view.

She heard a noise, turned to fire again, and saw Bloom slip past her. A large blue turquoise lion fetish which Rachael's grandfather had given him was hanging prominently outside his shirt around his neck.

Bloom leapt over the heap of bodies and blood to throw his arms around Rachael, who dropped her knife, tears flowing freely from both of them.

As he pulled Rachael closer, Bloom noted, "This is the second time you saved our lives. Boy, did I do something right when I married you."

Then, as if he were an angel, Pack slowly rose to his knees, covered in his tormenter's blood. "I'm OK, don't shoot," he said as he pushed Max's body off his own. He had a rare smile on his face. The bullet had never found its mark. His walking museum of rocks backpack had stopped its trajectory. "Figured I'd just play possum under the circumstances."

"Smart move," nodded Shirley.

Seeing Pack arise from the dead, the President, who was slumped over at this point, pulled out a #35 cab and handed it to Pack with his one semi-good arm, leaving a small drip pattern of blood trailing behind. "In case I bleed to death, I want you to have this. You earned it. You are truly a great stone man."

Then the President stumbled over to PC and collapsed as Simplton was untying her.

"Isn't it about time we get married? Call it an early birthday surprise," the President said to PC. "By the way, I finally think I'm in trouble as I'm madly in love with you and don't ever want to lose you again."

PC removed her own gag, choking back tears as she answered, "This trouble, I can handle. And yes, I will marry you. I always wanted to be a first lady. Now I'm ordering you not to die on me. We have a wedding to plan." She smiled at the love of her life and gave him a kiss gently on his parched lips.

Simplton realized she was seeing real love at close range. It was raw and powerful and affected her more than she wanted. Would she ever find companionship? Settle down with someone who cared about her more than life itself?

The sound of an FBI helicopter arriving overhead broke the moment of reflection and Officer Shirley Simplton returned to the present. She had a crime scene to supervise. Love would have to wait.

CHAPTER 57

WORLD FAMOUS MUSEUM

It had been five months since the ordeal. It was July now, with Indian Market fast approaching in Santa Fe. Bloom was caught up in his usual summertime frenzy of selling at his gallery, but he got frequent updates from Shirley and the stone men.

The deaths of Leroy, Blue, and Roscoe had been attributed to a greedy, power-hungry madman, Max Solenhosen. There were few details in the papers and nothing about the CXI corporation. The FBI wanted it that way, according to Simplton, who had confided in Bloom, apparently feeling she owed him the insider information considering what his family had gone through. The Bureau was now working with the CIA, the case an international affair. The fake Native jewelry that had gotten out on the market was of no interest to the Bureau at this point.

Bloom understood a case was being brought against Retieff Hearten by the Justice Department, and was being pursued through the South Africa courts. Simplton told him she had her doubts about prosecution on any crimes, since she had killed their only witness, Max Solenhosen, and it was unclear if the files taken by Preston could be used as evidence although they were quite helpful. Professor Heard had resigned quietly.

Max's body was retrieved under diplomatic status shortly after the shooting by a private plane flown in by CXI. The CXI mine near Crownpoint shut down operations temporarily. A company press release blamed a soft economy, but all indications were that the closure would become permanent as long as Retieff Hearten was under U.S. Internal Affairs scrutiny, a bargaining chip for later.

Shirley Simplton asked to extend her assignment in Santa Fe until the case was officially closed or shelved. Her desire to stay came from the urging of both Bloom and Rachel, who felt a deep gratitude to Shirley for risking her life to save Rachael and Preston. They were convinced that seeing Indian Market firsthand, and realizing what stopping the manufacture of fake jewelry meant to the life blood of the Native world, would give Shirley a renewed feeling for what family meant and maybe change the course of her life.

The Navajo Nation approved Hastiin Begay's request for a five-year contract for surface mining of #35 turquoise. No iridium or molybdenum extraction would be permitted. Mining was restricted to the first eight inches of topsoil. This stipulation would limit the amount of turquoise that could be found and assure that #35 would be the most valuable turquoise on the planet, since only a limited amount could ever be mined and all of it had a molybdenum matrix.

The President and Pack formed a corporation, Stone Men LLC. Pack's walking museum finally found a brick and mortar home with the help of the President's financial backing. A small storefront off old Highway 66 in Gallup was rented and furnished with turn-of-the-century display cases to house the contents of the famous Pack on the Back mini-museum, complete with a Navajo jewelry gift shop which PC, the new first lady, was running. The front sign was a wooden cutout of the Pack's backpack, juxtaposed against red metal lettering that read "World Famous Pack Turquoise Museum and Gift Shop."

Rachael's weaving, which had been savagely cut off her loom, was salvaged as best it could be and now had an honored place in the new Pack Turquoise Museum. The textile was displayed attached to a loom to show how tapestry weavings were made. A sign next to the weaving advertised Bloom's gallery website and its famous Toadlena weaver.

Besides opening a new museum, the two stone men were now the sole distributors of all #35 turquoise from Hastiin Begay's land for the next three years, a stipulation in the deal Begay had set up with the Navajo Nation. Begay also loaned his boyhood #35 jacula to the museum. A placard displayed with it described the rare turquoise and its owner's part in helping to bring the #35 mine to life. Hastiin Begay's son moved to Gallup to help run the mining operation. The old man's years of working with construction crews in LA would finally pay off. He had never been happier.

Roscoe's and Leroy's bodies were recovered at the power plant incinerator, which was not in operation since it had been shut off to comply with environmental regulations. Leroy's #35 stone was still in the pouch around his grossly swollen neck. Leroy's body was returned to his wife in Gallup. Roscoe, who had no family, was buried in a small cemetery near Toadlena.

Preston gave a lovely eulogy at the funeral and announced afterwards that when he finished his degree in two years he would be going into the family business of art as a silversmith, at least part time.

All the jewelry that had been bought with FBI money would be kept as evidence for now. Once the case was officially closed, Bloom had been granted permission to purchase it, excluding the fakes, at scrap value, providing Bloom's with a certain profit sometime down the road. One set of dangle earrings were already promised to his wife, a belated Valentine's gift.

Bloom confessed his undying love for Rachael the night after the rescue. He promised he would never keep secrets from her again, no matter the cost. And if she had to have another child, he was game.

Rachael was so moved by her husband's promise and compromise that she offered to move to Santa Fe for a period to see if it might help rejuvenate his career and make the feasibility of supporting a third child a reality. They would look for housing that could support a flock of sheep in August.

Bloom's Art Gallery was giving Preston his first show in place of Rachael's yearly Indian Market show. Rachael couldn't possibly get another large rug ready in time for the annual August event.

The President had given Preston 20 carats of #35 stones at a price well below wholesale for this show, as a thank you from Stone Men LLC. This all but guaranteed Preston a sellout for his first show as everyone wanted an example of #35 turquoise for their collection.

Both Preston and Billy Poh became Bloom's first silversmith artists. The gallery opened up a small jewelry section to complement the Native contemporary art and Rachel's weavings. Preston was working in a modern style in keeping with his late father Willard's path. Rachael approved and was thrilled.

The President magnanimously traded Rachael the last #35 cabochon that Leroy had cut in exchange for her damaged textile, suggesting that Preston make a bracelet highlighting the precious stone as a present for Rachael's bravery. The bracelet would be exhibited as "not for sale" during Preston's opening night reception at Bloom's, and thereafter would belong to Rachael.

Directly across from Rachael's rug in the museum was a special glass case with a small but exquisite four-carat stone which the President had purchased from Leroy's widow for $4,000, or $1,000 a carat, a record sale for a turquoise nugget. Underneath the illuminated stone was a large bronze plaque that read: "The first #35 stone ever cut and polished, by master lapidary Leroy Lancaster, a friend to all stone men."

The End

NEW NOVEL

BETWEEN THE WHITE LINES

BY MARK SUBLETTE

"There are some things you learn best in calm, and some in storm."
— Willa Cather, *The Song of the Lark* (1915)

CHAPTER 1

PING!

Hail pelted the front door's old broken screen, each plunk representing a lost dollar and the realization there would be no new shoes this spring, a yearly treat in the Hare household. The ice particles tearing the outside mesh announced unwelcome visitors to the family farm during harvest time. Nourishing rain is a godsend for a farmer; frozen water is God's special wrath. For the Hare family and their marginal wheat crop in the mid-1960s, it was the lord's payback. At least that was how Franklin saw it.

Mother Nature was looting the family's meager legacy and nothing short of a miracle could stop her destruction. The Hares' only source of income, the winter wheat crop, would soon be a total loss, the casualty of a colliding cold front and moist Gulf air on the high plains of Oklahoma. April was supposed to be the month of joy, one of the few decent times of the year that Franklin Hare remembered fondly. Most kids have treasured memories of Christmas or summer vacation. Franklin longed for April when the wheat crop came to market and money flowed.

And yet today, April 4th, marked a time of sorrow for Franklin. The number four would afterwards be cursed in his mind, representing pain and loss. Little could the young boy know that like the Japanese who consider four an unlucky number, his own *chi* was being doomed by critical inertia on this blustery day. Afterwards, a predetermined destiny would assume control of his existence, which would reach fruition only years later when once again God's wrath would make its presence felt.

Franklin's world as a child was one of fear and deprivation. He hated anything he could not control, especially Mother Nature's destructive powers. His existence was centered around an alcoholic mother and angry stepfather. His only source of stability was his half-brother Johnny. No pets were tolerated except livestock animals who he could love but would soon find turned into the dinner meal.

Outside, Johnny and their stepfather battled to save a portion of the winter crop, the old combine engine whining against the high-pitched ping of ice chips bouncing off the worn-out, rusted orange exterior. It was a lost cause and Franklin knew it. Franklin was fortunate today. His right arm was broken from a "family accident" so he was excused from heavy farm work. His work realm was the kitchen sink and bathrooms until his arm, with its spiral radial-head fracture, healed.

It's rare to be able to pinpoint when your life changes irrevocably, but at age 13, Franklin recognized that moment. He peered out the cracked kitchen window of the 100-year-old dilapidated farmhouse, and watched as the harvester sunk into the mud, almost buried, and hail filled all negative space. He watched as his brother Johnny dug frantically with his earth-encrusted hands to free the harvester's massive rear tires. Franklin marveled at the circus of marble-sized ice pebbles bouncing off his brother's steaming head. The frozen projectiles ricocheted in unexpected directions, each hit causing an involuntary twitch of pain, but their stepfather's anger was Johnny's primary concern, not the hail. If it wasn't for the serious danger his brother was facing, Franklin would have been rolling on the floor at the sight of such a spectacle, but he wasn't laughing.

Time slowed for Franklin. As the front-door screen's pitched battle slowly subsided, his own present dilemma intensified. He stood at the sink, frantically washing the multicolored dishes. Perfection was paramount. The distraction of cleaning the spotless Frankoma dishes helped focus his mind away from the forces of evil that would soon descend on the family dinner table. Franklin feared for Johnny, and for himself.

This test of God's humbling power could be the breaking point for a family on the edge. Franklin could only pray that the storm's fury would continue so he wouldn't have to face his father's rage. Bartholomew Hare, his stepfather, would probably depart his tractor's cab once he realized his crop was doomed, and his next stop would no doubt be the root cellar where he kept his high-grade moonshine, the only quality possession in the household. The night would be a dangerous place in or outside for all the Hare residents, broken arm or not.

As it turned out, farm life in Enid, Oklahoma, would soon be only a memory for the Hare family, and Franklin would never be the same.

To be continued in BETWEEN THE WHITE LINES, *scheduled for release in April 2015.*

Photography courtesy Mark Sublette, unless otherwise noted

Page 1:   *Dinosaur Egg Shaped Boulders,* Near Slot Canyon, Navajo Reservation
Page 5:   *Evening Sunset near Toadlena,* New Mexico
Page 15: *The Road into Toadlena,* New Mexico
Page 18: *Flame of Fire Ministries,* Gallup, New Mexico
Page 22: *Lawrence Baca's Lapidary Shop,* Santa Fe, New Mexico
Page 25: *Turnoff to Crownpoint,* Thoreau, New Mexico
Page 29: *Navajo Hogan Close Up,* Navajo Reservation
Page 32: *Medicine Man Gallery Courtyard,* 602A Canyon Road, New Mexico
Page 40: *Coming over La Bajada Hill into the Santa Fe Basin, Winter Time,* New Mexico
Page 45: *New Mexico's Finest,* Santa Fe Plaza
Page 60: *Grazing Sheep,* Shiprock on the Horizon near Toadlena
Page 65: *February 10th, New Stones Unpacked,* Tucson Gem and Mineral Show 2014, Arizona
Page 69: *Buckets of Stabilized Turquoise,* Tucson Gem and Mineral Show 2014, Arizona
Page 74: *Turquoise Cabochons,* Tucson Gem and Mineral Show 2014, Arizona
Page 77: *Trailer,* Gallup, New Mexico
Page 86: *Old Route 66,* Gallup, New Mexico
Page 89: *Lotaburger,* Gallup, New Mexico
Page 93: *Tire on Fence near Gallup,* New Mexico
Page 98: Navajo Jewelry Kit, courtesy Medicine Man Gallery
Page 104: Navajo Turquoise and Silver Dangle Earrings, circa 1940, courtesy Medicine Man Gallery
Page 122: *Anasazi Pottery Sherds,* Northern New Mexico
Page 135: *Shed,* Gallup, New Mexico
Page 142: *Incoming Storm,* Shiprock, New Mexico
Page 148: Roscoe's Note
Page 151: *Quick Mart, Highway 491, Turnoff to Toadlena,* New Mexico
Page 159: *Near Crownpoint,* New Mexico
Page 168: Jewelry Loop, courtesy Medicine Man Gallery
Page 179: *Holiday Inn,* Farmington, New Mexico
Page 183: *New Mexico Tech,* Soccorro, NM
Page 193: *Graffiti Watertank near the Navajo Nation*

Page 197: *Petroglyphs,* Northern New Mexico
Page 200: *Moonrise over Canyon*
Page 203: *Table Mesa in Dust Storm,* near Shiprock, New Mexico
Page 216: *Trading Post Sign*, Gallup, New Mexico

THE NAVAJO NATION

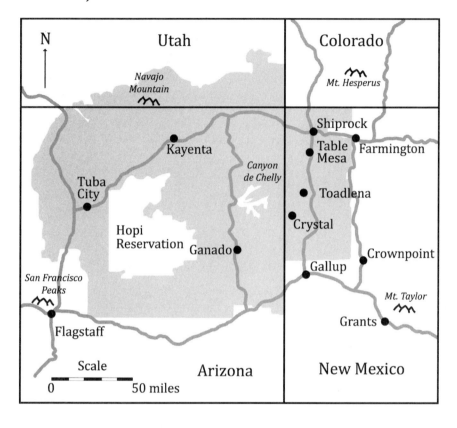